MW00770510

To Julie

# KENDAL THE BAKER BEE

BEE HAPPY

John Hartigan

# Kendal the Baker Bee

*A Fantasy for All Ages*

## JOHN A. HARTIGAN

Castle Keep Press
JAMES A. ROCK & COMPANY, PUBLISHERS
ROCKVILLE • MARYLAND

*Kendal the Baker Bee: A Fantasy for All Ages* by John A. Hartigan

CASTLE KEEP PRESS

is an imprint of JAMES A. ROCK & CO., PUBLISHERS

*Kendal the Baker Bee: A Fantasy for All Ages* copyright © 2007
by John A. Hartigan

Special contents of this edition copyright ©2007
by James A. Rock & Co., Publishers

*Address comments and inquiries to:*
CASTLE KEEP PRESS
James A. Rock & Company, Publishers
9710 Traville Gateway Drive, #305
Rockville, MD 20850
**E-mail:**
jrock@rockpublishing.com    lrock@rockpublishing.com
Internet URL: www.rockpublishing.com

ISBN: 978-1-59663-788-7
1-59663-788-9

Library of Congress Control Number: 2007923657

Printed in the United States of America

First Edition: 2007

*For Jean*

*the love of my life*

# Acknowledgments

My appreciation to Jean, my dear wife for forty-seven years. Her ideas and edits of the countless rewrites were invaluable. Her spark, encouragement and insightful criticism carried me through to the final version.

Gratitude too is due my readers ... daughter Joan Mary, CSJ; son John; Joan Lewis O. Carm; and Marguerite Lewis, SBS.

Thanks also to other readers: Richard Del Belso, Ellen Hallen, Karen Pandell, Edna Karp, Andy Kort, and Lois Lewis. Special thanks to Kay Rogler for editing the manuscript.

I forget you not, Father Christian Aidan Carr, OCSO, Trappist monk and dear friend, formerly editor of the *National Homiletics Journal.*

To Frank Hodge, proprietor of Hodge Podge Books and life-long devotee to good children's literature, my thanks for your kind remonstrations, to write ... write and write over again.

Lastly, to Lilda Rock Wiley, daughter of my publisher, thanks for discovering Kendal among four thousand queries, to give him the chance to share his story in print.

Note to readers: Patsy Morris sketched the Kendal pictures thirty-five years ago and I've lost track of her whereabouts. But thank you Patsy.

# Celebrating Beekeepers

Only in researching honey bees for *Kendal the Baker Bee* was the author introduced to beekeeping, a food production method dating back to 13,000 BC. In the United States 125,000 beekeepers—whether full-time entrepreneurs, sideliners or hobbyists—manage colonies using their hands, hearts and heads to ensure the health, happiness and productivity of their honeybees. Millions of beekeepers throughout the world apply the same dedication including 13,000 in Canada, 45,000 in Mexico and 600,000 in China.

Beekeepers practice their art with fortitude and determination. On the front lines in open country or in their own back yards, they perform a long list of tasks: building and repairing beehives, transporting, inserting and removing honeycombs, controlling bee diseases and parasites, packaging and selling honey and other hive products.

There are many forces frustrating beekeepers in their labors. Presently, a mysterious ailment called Colony Collapse Disorder is wiping out large numbers of colonies in twenty-seven states. But the 125,000 beekeepers persevere.

Commercial beekeepers try to meet the needs of crop growers who depend heavily on honey bees to pollinate 90 cultivated flowering crops—apples, almonds, cranberries and watermelons to name only four. Beekeepers gather and process other hive products: honey in its purest form or in combination with other ingredients for popular cereals and bread. In addition, pollen and royal jelly are used for medicinal and nutritional purposes and beeswax in making candles, cosmetic products and wood polish.

The job of beekeeper is a lonely calling. It involves working in isolated areas for long and irregular hours, requires immunity from bee stings, the ability to lift heavy objects and an interest in botany (plants) and entomology (insects).

We owe beekeepers our gratitude for the work they do.

—*John A. Hartigan*

The pedigree of honey
Does not concern the bee;
A clover, any time, to him
Is aristocracy.

—*Emily Dickinson*

# Chapter One

# First Things First

Queen Zoey was running out of time. This afternoon she broke the all-time honey bee record, but tonight she tossed and turned. Laying 500,000 eggs was a remarkable achievement for an ordinary queen bee. But Zoey wasn't ordinary. She was the last in a long line of queen bees who possessed the power of royal longevity—the ability to live a thousand years.

The power was successfully passed on by all Zoey's 303 queen bee ancestors when they laid a special *fertilized* egg. Continuation of the line of succession now depended on her. No more delays. She would do her duty tomorrow.

Long before dawn, Zoey arose and tapped her assistant, Rebecca, on the shoulder. They made their way along a path between towering honeycombs until the Queen found a suitable clean cell. She asked Rebecca to wait as she entered and did her duty.

"Oh, no … no!" Zoey cried. "This is not right. I laid an *unfertilized* egg. I failed my test (the Queen knew an unfertilized egg is a male bee). The royal line of succession is broken."

"What will you do, my queen?" Rebecca asked.

"Why, raise my son, of course. He's a blessing. I predict he will do great things in the world of bees. You'll see. Now, I need a boy's name. Help me, Rebecca."

"I'm sorry, your highness. I can list a thousand girls' names. But I don't have one boy's name on the tip of my tongue."

"Then I'll call him Kendal. The name has a ring about it." With her shoulders straight and her head held high, Zoey returned to the business of laying more eggs.

*** 

Three days later, Kendal emerged as a larva, half the size of a grain of rice. He was shapeless without legs or wings. His mouth wagged greedily for something to eat. Soon Kendal grew strong enough to play tag with the other drones. He listened as the older guys told him how female worker bees considered all drones lazy, worthless oafs. Kendal didn't believe anyone was worthless. He'd change the females' minds, somehow.

After three weeks of laying eggs, Queen Zoey sent for Kendal. She missed seeing her newest son. Kendal proceeded through a maze of honey combs on his way to her chamber.

Oops! Kendal near tripped over a drone named Tee. As they untangled their six legs, Kendal stood up. Tee refused to stand. He lived up to his reputation as a troublemaker. Reluctantly, Kendal apologized and said, "Good morning."

"What's good about it?" Tee rejoined as he wagged his head in disgust. "Today is another dull day with no work to do. I'm tired of sitting around idly."

Tee ticked off his complaints without waiting for Kendal to agree or disagree. Kendal understood drones were considered un-productive members of the colony, but he had his own ideas.

"A drone can always find work to do in a busy hive. It's up to us to find our niche," Kendal said. "Better days are coming. You'll see."

Tee shrugged. He didn't believe anyone was able to change a drone's boring life.

As Kendal made his way upstairs to Queen Zoey's chamber,

he peeked inside. A set of glowing eyes stared at him. "I see you, Kendal. My, how you've grown."

Zoey beamed as she inspected Kendal's appearance. She saw a handsome lad, stout of frame, almost as big as she. His unusually large green eyes distinguished him from the other drones.

Kendal rubbed his eyes, blinking repeatedly as he examined his mother's physique. Her body resembled a wasp's with a long slender frame and short wings.

Queen Zoey realized Kendal was now old enough to go to work; worker bees by three weeks old were producing wax and repairing broken honey combs. Zoey worried about her son's future because drones ages ago, gave up searching for work. She was determined for Kendal to learn a trade.

"Kendal, if you had your choice, what job interests you?"

Kendal didn't hesitate. He'd become a baker bee. Honey cakes, muffins and bread would provide a variety in the worker bees' diet. Kendal's choice didn't surprise Queen Zoey. Fortunately, an unused bakery in the basement of the hive was molding away. The location was an ideal place to set up a business. And so, Zoey decided to send him to baking school.

Zoey thought Kendal was now old enough to keep a secret— that he was born a royal prince. Kendal gulped as Zoey's words lodged like a lump in his throat. The title of prince didn't faze him. But to be called prince … "yes, prince … no, prince" … that bothered him. He was satisfied being an ordinary drone.

With one secret uncorked, Zoey shared a second one. An old oak tree near their hive appeared dead on the outside. Inside, 303 queens bustled about their daily activities. Kendal and Rebecca stared at each other in disbelief.

"Come closer, please," Queen Zoey beckoned to Kendal and Rebecca. She saved the best secret for last—she was the youngest in line behind 303 older queens. Zoey intended to retire soon to live with the other retirees who possessed the power of royal longevity. That was her destiny.

"Someday, you both must fly by the dead old oak tree and see for yourselves," Zoey said. "I'm sure you'll spot at least one queen wearing a long beard."

Rebecca confessed that one day she noticed an old queen pacing nonchalantly on a limb of the old oak tree. The old bee wore a long white beard wrapped around her stomach five times. Yes, five times; Rebecca counted twice. She thought she was hallucinating. She decided not to report the incident. No one would believe her.

"Rebecca, you saw Queen Victoria. She's the eldest queen. She founded the hive four hundred years ago here in Virginia. To this day, Victoria claims responsibility for starting the royal line of succession, on the very day she laid the first royal egg."

***

Even as Zoey mentioned her name, Queen Victoria strolled into view on her favorite limb of the old oak tree. Completely relaxed, she squatted on a bump to talk with two other retirees, Queen Mame and Queen Dame. They were assigned permanent day shift as guards at the hive entrance.

"Listen, Mame. Quiet," Dame whispered as she pointed at a noise she heard beneath the limb. "We have company on the ground."

Queen Victoria cocked her head to listen. She asked Dame, "What's making that racket below?" Victoria's eyesight was deteriorating more every day; her hearing was far less than perfect.

Quietly, Dame eased toward the edge of the limb and peered over the side. "Shush. There's no problem, Victoria," Dame assured her; "It's only a young girl and boy sitting on the grass."

"How old are they, Dame?"

"I'd say very old, Victoria … maybe eleven for the girl and eight for the boy."

Dame overheard the children discussing the boy's beagle hound. They said he went crazy outdoors. Today he ran off to chase rabbits.

"Watch out," the girl yelled as a field bee buzzed her ear, flying behind the tree. She ducked as two more field bees buzzed her head. Those two followed the same path as the first one.

Queen Dame worried the children might discover the rear entrance to the retirement hive. Only the old queens and worker bees making deliveries knew about the hive's back door.

The girl and boy searched every inch of the trunk, even in the notches of the bark of the old oak tree. They found no trace of the three bees.

Finally, the kids gave up their search and separated. The girl returned home to help her mother, a beekeeper who cared for 140 hives surrounding her home. The little boy ran into the woods to find his pal beagle.

# Chapter Two

# Off On His Own

Zoey considered her options. There was an unused bakery standing empty in the basement. On the other hand, the queens' retirement hive prided itself having a master baker on premises. Why not send Kendal there for training? Kendal jumped at the idea of going to bakery school.

The Queen questioned Rebecca if Kendal's wings were strong enough to fly on his own. Rebecca nodded her head yes, saying, "By morning, Kendal will be fit to fly under his own power."

Since he needed directions to find the old oak tree, Zoey suggested Kendal go upstairs to her chamber. From that height, one can survey the outside world. The large oak tree was a real old timer ... four hundred years old. It no longer sprouted foliage on its well worn bare limbs. Only birds used it to rest their weary wings. As Kendal started to leave, he was cautioned by Zoey to be careful; he wasn't quite ready to fly on his flimsy wings.

Kendal climbed the stairs. He passed dozens of honey combs, each one constructed expertly. They stood straight up as library books do on their shelves. Kendal smiled with pride as he admired the bees' handiwork. Rebecca told him how the worker bees made so much honey that Zoey's hive had a surplus of 40 pounds in its stores.

As Kendal tiptoed on a deck outside the chamber, he inched ever nearer the edge. Kendal's large eyes fixed on the spectacular scene spreading out as far as one can see. A gust of wind whipped up suddenly. Its force lifted him like a feather, tossing him over the side.

Down, down, down, Kendal dropped, grappling to grip the air. His wings flapped clumsily trying to break his fall. Crash … Awkwardly he tumbled as he hit the ground, smack hard. Stunned, Kendal tested his wings, legs and antennae … nothing broken. Fortunately, the soft grass padded his fall.

As he stood up, Kendal heard a rustling noise in the grass; it startled him. Swish … swish; the sound resembled the warning issued by a coiled rattle snake ready to lunge at its victim.

"Oh, no!" Kendal yelled. A gruff-looking creature on thin, wobbly legs came sneaking out of the tall grass. He crept toward Kendal on eight legs, watching the drone with eight eyes, smacking two jaws with sharp fangs. Even when Kendal closed both eyes, he wasn't able to blot out the horrible sight.

"Little bee," the spider screamed. "Open your darn eyes. You stay right there. Don't you dare, move. Sticking you won't take me long; it won't hurt too much when I sting you. Trust me."

"Leave me alone, please," Kendal pleaded.

"Stop complaining. I'm coming right over."

A faint sound behind him caught Kendal's ear. Lumbering out of the thick grass, a large bushy creature inched forward. With movements resembling folding and unfolding of an accordion, its progress was *slooow*. Wearing a shiny green and gold speckled coat, the creature crawled forward. She propelled her dark green body on sixteen legs working in tandem. This thing, whatever its name, confronted the spider face to face.

"Scram," the thing blared out. "Get, get, before I get mad."

The thing's face was ugly, outrageously so. Its breath offensive. Kendal held his breath. The spider lost no time. He beat it as fast as his spindly legs carried him into the grass. But he hollered, "You haven't seen the end of me. Remember my name. It's Spero, spelled S-p-e-r-o."

Although he was a timid juvenile, Kendal showed no fear of this green 'whatever you call it.'

"Who are you?" Kendal asked.

"I'm a caterpillar."

"Do you have a name?"

"My name's Greeney the Caterpillar. I'm a monarch caterpillar. What's your name, little bee?"

"It's Kendal. You're kind, Greeney, to stop by to help me," Kendal said with relief. "Where do you live?"

"I'm an orphan, temporarily," Greeney answered. "I live in the bark of your tree. I'm making my rounds to eat milkweed leaves, nibbling on as many as I can find. What are you doing outside your hive?"

"I fell from a limb."

Kendal sized up the caterpillar as a neat lady. She was likeable, even with her grotesque face. Kendal decided to share his plans. He told Greeney he hoped to start baking classes the next day, if his wings were strong enough.

"That's a great trade. I wish I knew how to bake," Greeney said.

An idea popped into Kendal's head. With Greeney's long, firm, broad back, she might help in the bakery. He needed help, mixing batter and transporting bakery products throughout the hive. So he asked Greeney if she wanted a job.

Greeney reared up on her hind quarters to prove her agility, ready to go to work. But worries bugged her; the other bees might object having a stranger in their hive. Kendal didn't see a problem, but first he must find his way back up the tree.

The small boy chasing his beagle crashed through the trees.

Startled to find a bee and a caterpillar yakking as close friends, he stopped a few feet away. In a calm voice, the boy told the insects not to fear; he prized every creature in the forest.

Both Kendal and Greeney heard the boy's voice clearly. They even understood his words as he knelt down. If he fell over on them, they expected to be splashed like a fly walloped by a fly swatter.

The boy flopped down on his stomach. Eye to eye he inspected the insects. Kendal found the boy's face fascinating … round and smooth, curly, blond hair … a smile to make you smile. The boy's mouth captured Kendal's attention, two mammoth front teeth, others of many shades and shapes and new ones sprouting out of empty spaces.

A beagle burst from the bushes, ready to frolic and play. The boy yelled. "Heydog! No … Stop … Sit."

*Marvel of marvels,* Kendal thought. A few words brought the large brown and white beast with his ears almost touching the ground, to a dead stop. Greeney was curious about the name of the dog. As if the little boy read Greeney's mind, he explained how he named his dog. When his parents bought the puppy, the boy tried six different names. Nothing worked. He didn't respond to Rover, Spud, Winston or any of the other names suggested. The answer dawned. When the boy yelled, "hey, dog," the puppy came. And so the beagle got his name, Heydog.

"Heydog, come," called the boy. He allowed the beagle hound to approach … not too close.

Before Heydog stepped on the fragile insects, the boy commanded … "Stop."

Heydog responded, sitting down on cue. The boy told the insects his name was Aidan, son of local beekeepers who maintained 140 hives not far away.

Aidan liked Kendal's looks. Never had he seen a drone with dark green eyes; the other drones had purplish brown eyes. Kendal indeed was different. The little drone appeared too young to fly back to his hive. He said it out loud. "If the caterpillar let Kendal hitch a ride on his back, the caterpillar might carry the bee up the tree." Without even a nod they understood. Kendal mounted on Greeney's long back. As he sunk into the soft body, she undertook the rough climb through the notches of the tree bark.

Aidan remained on the ground watching their slow progress, clapping his hands in encouragement. *They liked my idea,* Aidan thought to himself. He sighed with relief as the young drone made his way home.

As they climbed higher, Aidan yelled. "Come and visit me tomorrow, little drone. You travel in a straight line from here, past the old oak tree ... keep going north ... over the hill ... you'll see my house, the first one with white shutters."

Kendal said goodbye to Greeney at the hive entrance, offering his gratitude. He promised Greeney a job starting the following afternoon about dinner time. Kendal believed Queen Zoey would allow a caterpillar to work in the hive. She encouraged every bee to work.

As Kendal said goodbye to Greeney, Tee lurked nearby, out of sight. Tee had overheard what the boy said. Tee also watched how Kendal played chummy with the boy. Tee filed away his suspicions for another time.

When challenged at the hive's entrance by the guards, Kendal complimented them. No one passed them without the necessary security check. They verified Kendal's scent as a familiar one and allowed him to enter. In these treacherous days with killer bees on the rampage, the guards were instructed by Rebecca to exercise great care. A short time ago, a killer bee scout tried to bait the guards to let her go inside. The guards arrested the killer bee and placed her in a holding cell.

✳✳✳

Queen Zoey was mortified early this morning when she detected a new irritation. Her face turned scarlet when whiskers showed on her chin. Rebecca heard Zoey yell. She hurried over to calm the Queen, reassuring her pollen powder hides whiskers. Queen Zoey knew better. These shoots indicated the first signs of a beard in the making. As she rubbed the bristles, trying to make them disappear, Kendal appeared at her side.

"Mother, you won't believe what happened," Kendal exclaimed. "I didn't try to fly. I fell from the balcony. I met a caterpillar and a young boy under the tree."

"Are you hurt?" Rebecca inquired with concern.

Kendal answered he was fine. He'd like to rest a bit but first he had a request for Queen Zoey. "Mother, may I invite a caterpillar to come inside the hive to work with me in the bakery?"

Without hesitating, Queen Zoey approved Kendal's request with one stipulation. Greeney must watch where she wandered. To prevent the worker bees from getting excited, Zoey decided to issue an advisory to the colony. The workers should not fear a caterpillar called Greeney when she visited the hive tomorrow. She was the Queen's guest.

Zoey knew the baking instructor expected recommendations for trainees. So she handed Kendal a letter of introduction and a personal note. With proper credentials, he was guaranteed a training spot when he visited the old oak tree in the morning.

Zoey was certain Queen Leah, Kendal's grandmother, would take good care of him when he arrived for training. As a sign of her affection, Queen Zoey leaned down to give Kendal a peck on his cheek. She wished him good luck in baker's school, the only one of its kind in the forest.

# Chapter Three

# A Baker Bee For Real

Before the birds peeped their good day to each other, Kendal primed his body for his solo flight. Limbering up untested wings, he stretched like a long distance runner preparing to compete in a marathon.

With one mighty thrust, Kendal launched himself into the wide blue yonder. Using the power of four wings, he maneuvered around trees and tall bushes blocking his path. Down, down, he dove to test his reflexes. Up, up he soared to measure the length and width of the sky. With confidence Kendal aimed for the big old oak tree.

Flying over the fields, Kendal sadly viewed the blotched acres with dry hay waiting for harvesting. The area was a tinder box ready to ignite. As he passed above the underbrush, he noticed two hunters hiding in a tree; they waited to shoot their quota of deer. *Oh no,* he thought, *one hunter smoking near the hay field.*

At the retirement hive entrance, a large queen brushed aside her long shiny white beard.

"Good morning. You're Kendal, aren't you?" the queen bee greeted him.

"Yes, and you're Queen Leah, right?"

"Yes, little feller. What a surprise, Kendal. I never dreamed to see my royal grandson coming to visit his old grandmother. Come over here; give me a big kiss."

Kendal noticed the family resemblance immediately. Kendal handed Queen Leah the letter of introduction and the personal note from his mother.

"Can you read the letter to me, Kendal? My eyes aren't as sharp as yours."

Kendal unfolded the scrap and read out loud.

*Dear Mother,*

*May I present Kendal, your royal grandchild? He does our family proud. Kendal is intelligent and articulate. Please teach him how to become a baker bee for my colony. I know your hive has the best bakery chef living with you.*

*Mother Leah, you have reason to be proud of our royal prince. Kendal knows how to make friends; he has two new ones, Greeney the Caterpillar and a young boy by the name of Aidan.*

*I'll retire soon. I plan to live with you and the royal queens for a thousand years to come. Thanks for your help.*

*With love, Zoey*

Queen Leah complimented Kendal on his reading skills. To assign a newcomer to a spot in the baking school required clearance with the Queens' Council. Leah also must check the chef's schedule. So she excused herself, leaving Kendal with the guards.

Kendal looked around. "I don't see any guards," Kendal said as doubt clouded his face.

"That's the idea," Queen Leah responded. "Here but not here. I'll call them—Mame … Dame … come, show yourselves; meet my handsome grandson Kendal."

Two strapping queen bees appeared, dressed in camouflaged trench coats. Both sported long white shiny beards. Mame wore a badge, number 108; Dame wore number 188.

"This is Kendal," Leah said. "He's visiting us. While I do a clearance check, please give him an orientation to our hive. We keep no secrets from Kendal."

Mame spoke first. "Welcome, Kendal. What would you like to know?"

"Everything ... I'm only kidding," Kendal replied. "You two certainly look in wonderful shape for—you know what I mean?"

"Old ladies," Mame added. "I can say what I think. You're too polite, Kendal."

Kendal learned that Mame and Dame wrestled in their spare time. They both graduated as martial arts experts, earning black belts. In addition, they wore the same size badges as the other queens in the retirement hive.

Dame told Kendal each number specified the order in which the queens retired and arrived at the old oak tree hive. For example, Queen Leah's badge read 303 as the newest retiree in the hive. Queen Victoria wore badge number 1. She established the original colony for retirees.

Kendal bit his tongue as he tried to resist asking more questions. It might appear rude. *Oh well,* he thought ... and he went on. He asked why their skin appeared as rough as shoe leather. Did that come with age?

"Yes and no," Mame replied. She explained their skin thickened over time, turning hard as a callous. Not even a bee stinger punctured their skin.

The orientation continued with Mame taking the lead. When the hive was designed, it was built as a fortress with a massive hallway with interior high walls reaching as high as the ceiling. Only one door led into the Council's meeting room. In the event an enemy broke into the hive, the great hallway easily converted into a holding area to trap an enemy. If the oak wood door slammed shut near the front entrance, any invaders would be trapped inside the hall with no way to escape.

Mame told Kendal the queens slept upstairs. On the lower level, there was a dining room, an exercise room, a beauty shop, a bakery and a library. They were arranged in a line as stores are in a shopping mall. Because Queen Zoey's hive didn't have a beauty shop or a library, Kendal asked why the queens needed two specialty areas.

"There's a simple explanation," Mame said. "The queens visit the beauty shop to have their beards shaped. Queen Victoria visits every other day to get a trim and have her beard wound around her stomach."—

"Five times, right?" interjected Kendal. "I heard about her."

"Yes, you're right, Kendal." There was a story circulating through the hive that Queen Victoria pledged to let her beard grow indefinitely, unless she became convinced to cut it off.

Dame explained that the library housed one thousand honey recipes. "Let me recite the titles for you—"

With a rustling of her robe, Queen Leah hurried down the hallway. "I'm sorry for the interruption, Kendal. But the Council invites you to make an appearance."

Queen Victoria was presiding over the meeting as Leah and Kendal arrived. Victoria stopped in mid-sentence to offer Leah and Kendal a warm welcome.

"Come in, come right in," Queen Victoria greeted their guest. "Welcome, Prince Kendal, to the Queens' Council meeting."

Each retiree eyed the young drone. They rustled their wings vigorously in welcome. Standing at the lectern, Victoria beckoned for Leah and Kendal to join her.

"Kendal, as you arrived, we heard a marvelous report. Our colony has a surplus inventory of 700 pounds of honey. Isn't that superb?"

Kendal couldn't imagine so much honey in one hive. He heard Queen Zoey's hive had a surplus of 40 pounds, a record for her colony. But 700 pounds took up a huge amount of space. He didn't think it possible for retirees to store such a large quantity of honey in their retirement hive. Victoria guarded her secret; but she willingly shared it with Kendal.

Fifty years ago Queen Victoria visualized the project. She assigned carpenter bees to hollow out the bottom of the old oak tree and bore holes through the bark to make tunnels with a swinging door going outside. Delivery of supplies to the retirees was made easy. The back door was used as an emergency exit. With enlarged storage facilities, there was no problem providing storage space for 700 pounds of honey.

Victoria paused for a long breath. *Enough said for today,* she thought. She invited Kendal to speak to the Council.

Public speaking was a new experience for him. He forced his lips to move. He told the queens he appreciated the invitation to learn baking techniques. What more was there to say at this time? So Kendal thanked them for listening.

Queen Victoria thought the young drone acted confidently. She cautioned him to watch out for killer bees as he departed for home later. Recent reports indicated killer bees prowled through the forest, aching for trouble.

Kendal followed Leah through the hive facilities. They stopped at the beauty parlor which was open seven days a week. Peering inside, a stack of shelves was filled with memorabilia—the queens' keepsakes.

Queen Leah pointed out a tiny gold box kept on the top shelf. It belonged to Queen Victoria, but its contents remained a deep mystery.

A fragrant honey aroma acted as a beacon, to draw Leah and Kendal toward the bakery. They entered, coming up behind a queen bee who was engrossed in mixing a cake batter. Dressed in a full length white apron, the queen wiped off colored splotches on her apron. Even her body showed the spoils of cooking as if she had the measles. When the queen sensed Leah and Kendal behind her, she turned with a smile on her face.

"Hello, Leah," Martha said, "I'm pleased to have visitors to my kitchen."

"Kendal, this is our supreme chef, Queen Martha," Leah said. "May I present my grandson, Kendal? He needs lessons to become a baker bee."

Queen Martha didn't hesitate. She cleared a table. Enrolling her first male student was exciting. Martha had two hours to spare for a baking lesson.

After Leah said goodbye, Martha invited Kendal to join her at the large work table. She explained the procedure to bake honey products. She emphasized ... to stick with the basics ... to follow the recipe; she repeated her instructions three times.

When they finished preparing twelve pans of baked goods, they popped them into the oven. Martha wiped her brow—"Whew, Kendal!" Martha exclaimed as she shook the pollen dust from her body.

"Your system makes baking easy. You're a master teacher, Queen Martha. Using your recipes gives me confidence. I'm sure I can be a super baker bee."

Martha gave Kendal a collection of her ten favorite recipes and a backpack to wear wherever he traveled. Next, she extracted a crumbly soiled old document from a drawer. Carefully she unfolded the dried old paper, telling Kendal the paper contained the most prized recipe of the royal family.

Martha explained that the ingredients produced miracle cakes with medicinal benefits. The cakes warded off dangerous mites, which ravaged bee colonies. Kendal was flabbergasted. Imagine the queens entrusted him with a recipe that worked the same as a miracle drug. Queen Martha even gave him six sample miracle cakes to add to his backpack.

"Awesome," Kendal responded as Queen Martha shared the queens' treasures with him. Martha informed him the Council wished him to use the recipe for the benefit of bees all over the world.

Martha wasn't quite finished. She handed Kendal a certificate of achievement made out to 'Kendal the Baker Bee.' And finally, she presented him with a fluffy white baker's hat; it fit perfectly. Queen Martha even slipped six extra hats into the backpack for Kendal to award to others he trained as baker bees.

"How can I repay you, Queen Martha, for your kindness?" Kendal asked.

"Pass on what you've learned to other bees," Martha replied. "That's thanks enough. What's next on your agenda, Kendal?"

If Kendal hurried, he told her, he might have time to visit a boy named Aidan. He had invited Kendal to his house for a visit.

As he retraced his steps upstairs, Kendal passed Mame and Dame. They were engaged in practicing wrestling holds but stopped for a moment to wish him well. Outside, Queen Leah waited.

"Hi, Grandma. Thanks to you I'm a baker bee," Kendal said with pride.

"I see your white fluffy hat slipping out of your backpack. Pack it tightly and buckle the flap."

Kendal secured the flap. Going to a friend's house for the first time intrigued him. He didn't know what to expect. A two mile flight provided plenty of time to test his wings; those 140 bee hives surrounding Aidan's house might contain hostile bees. Maybe Aidan's family was home; Kendal never met humans except for Aidan. What would people thing about a stranger bee coming on their property, he wondered. He would find out, the hard way, very soon.

Chapter Four

# In The Front Door

Kendal licked his front leg; he raised it high in the air to test the wind currents. Up, up, he soared … he was on his way. Glancing down, he saw those same deer hunters doing nothing but tree sitting. He glided down for a better view—the urge for mischief too strong a temptation. He gave in. He buzzed the hunters noisily. One tried to swat him. Kendal caught a whiff of smoke as it curled around him. Ugh! He made a bee line for the fresh air.

As he winged his way above the forest, Kendal saw a dark brown mass coming toward him. Only by swerving aside did he miss a head on crash. As the swarm swirled by, it landed near the top of a birch tree.

Further on, Kendal laid eyes on a house with white shutters. The house appeared inviting except for a large village of bee hives surrounding the house. Kendal worried how Aidan's bees would react to a stranger visiting the yard.

It didn't take long to learn the truth. Aidan's bees resented intruders with a passion. Guard bees launched from ten hives to pursue him. Three times Kendal tried to approach the house. Three times the bees intercepted him to chase him off their property. With his strength sapped, Kendal made one last effort. He broke through their ranks, landing with a thud on the front porch. Exhausted and panting for breath, Kendal collapsed.

Aidan ran to the porch to see why the bees buzzed so loudly. Accidentally, he dropped his peanut butter sandwich. As he looked down, he stared. "Shoo, what happened?" he yelled, as he saw Kendal sitting on the floor, laboring to breathe.

"Little drone, you'd better come inside and rest yourself," Aidan said.

Kendal climbed on top of the sandwich, careful to avoid the gooey peanut butter. Aidan carried him to the kitchen table. He remembered his manners and placed a napkin underneath the sandwich. Next he fetched a jar of honey; he scooped out a bit on a spoon and set it near his tiny new friend.

At first, Kendal shrunk back. The smell of honey was too overpowering. As it dribbled down his chin, the sound of a door opening startled Kendal. He measured the height of the newcomer. A mighty tall lady dressed in jeans.

"That's my mom. Mrs. Bright," Aidan said.

Mrs. Bright didn't believe her eyes, a drone licking a spoon at her kitchen table. She never minded Aidan's insect friends. Her eight year old son often brought them home.

"Well, who do we have here?" noticing that Aidan provided a napkin.

"He's my new friend, Mom. Remember? I told you about him and the caterpillar."

"Of course I remember, Aidan." Mrs. Bright recalled the story about a bee and a caterpillar. When Aidan first told his mother the tale, she had her doubts. With a drone eating lunch at the kitchen table, Mrs. Bright knew Aidan's story was no exaggeration.

Kendal appreciated Mrs. Bright's hospitality. She relaxed on a kitchen chair after coming indoors from working the hives—a full time job keeping up with 140 hives of busy bees producing honey. She asked Aidan to excuse himself to go find Kim to have dinner. Mrs. Bright said the little drone might stay as long as he wanted. So Aidan left, the door open just in case.

After Aidan left to find Kim, Kendal became increasingly uncomfortable. He wasn't pleased sitting alone, next to a sandwich on a napkin. And Mrs. Bright was busy setting the table and preparing dinner. As she peeled potatoes, she whistled a tune. She expected a response from the canary jockeying for a better position in his cage. He didn't disappoint her. The chipper bird piped out a medley of long warbles. He even tried to drown out the noisy telephone ringing over and over.

Mrs. Bright ran to pick up the phone, cradling it under her chin. "Hi, Ron. I'm glad to hear from you ... Yes, Bill's still out to sea on the air craft carrier. The kids can't wait to have their father come home ... Yes, Ron, I'm concerned too. Our finances are in a shambles ... You're right. Losing our home is a possibility."

Kendal found it awkward, listening to a private conversation. As a distraction, he walked around the edge of the napkin. As the canary persisted to peep and chirp, Kendal chimed in. He found a new voice of his own—hmm ... hmm. At first he hummed quietly, soon loudly with gusto. Literally, he found himself humming in cadence with the warbling notes of the canary's song.

Kendal overheard Mrs. Bright say, "Honestly, Ron, our bees work as hard as they can. I can't remove more honey from their hives. What they store in their hives, they'll need when winter arrives in a few months.

Kendal became itchy; he flew over to visit the canary. With precision, he landed on the feeder attached to the cage; the canary didn't flinch. Rather, the yellow bird hopped sideward across his perch to stare directly into Kendal's large green eyes.

Nonchalantly, the canary pecked at seed in the feeder and spit out the shells; he was unafraid. He felt perfectly safe behind bars. Once in awhile, Aidan gave him a break and let him fly about the kitchen under supervision.

As Mrs. Bright continued explaining her financial problems to Ron, the canary leaked what he knew about her troubles to Kendal. Living in the kitchen provided the ideal place to eavesdrop on family conversations. Unless Mrs. Bright found some immediate relief, she might lose the home.

Only last night, Mrs. Bright flipped through her stack of bills, far too many due at the same time. While she worked on her checkbook, the canary heard Mrs. Bright comment. "If only I had another 500 pounds of honey to sell, I'd be able to pay these bills."

Hearing Mrs. Bright wrapping up her telephone conversation, the canary stopped his chatter to listen.

"Yes, Ron ... I do have one option. It might work. Sell the parcel of property we own, two miles from here. The lumber company made me an offer. They're interested in harvesting the trees for lumber. Unfortunately, the land includes my favorite tree, a four hundred year old oak ... I can show you the property if you want to see it. How's ten o'clock in the morning, day after tomorrow? ... No thanks, Ron. We don't need a ride. I promised the kids an outing. We'll come by wagon ... Great. I'll see you there. Bye."

*Aha, I have a plan,* she thought. Mrs. Bright lightened up, whistling in earnest. She noticed Kendal keeping company with the canary. She thought they made a cute pair, one peeping and the other humming in harmony.

Kendal sensed the pressures of the moment. With a worried frown, he told the canary he must leave for home. He hoped to find a solution to the money problems. But the deadline was tight, two days away ... 10:00 a.m., day after tomorrow.

With the exuberance of youth, Aidan barged into the kitchen with Kim trailing behind him. Kendal flapped his wings in relief. He lifted up, circled the children, humming in his new found voice as he flew about the kitchen. He pecked Aidan on the nose and flew out the door.

Aidan picked up six tiny nuggets sitting near the spoon on the table. They resembled ingots of gold, but not solid as real metal. Earlier Aidan saw the drone drop these tiny hunks on the kitchen table.

Aidan called his mother to show her what he found. His drone friend must have left the nuggets as a gift. She used a magnifying glass—*quite unusual,* she thought. She spent most of her life as a bee keeper and never saw anything to compare with these tiny gold hunks of something. She planned to take them to a professor at the University to be analyzed.

Kendal stopped at the top of the porch steps as he recalled his incoming flight. He swiveled his head this way and that, to check for danger before taking off. There were excellent reasons to fear trouble.

Heydog kept both eyes on the drone as he took his nap in the corner of the porch. He remembered seeing the drone only yesterday with a caterpillar. In a low bass voice, Heydog suggested he might help the drone work out his dilemma. Kendal couldn't guess how a beagle that chased rabbits might possibly scare off angry bees. But Heydog insisted; he had his share of experiences with bees as he nosed around the 140 hives.

Heydog had a secret weapon. He knew people ducked for cover when he sounded off with his penetrating loud voice, called tonguing. The hive guard bees didn't appreciate that much noise either. After an animated conversation, Kendal and Heydog worked out an arrangement.

As soon as Heydog started to run down the path through the hives, Kendal was to count one, two, and three … and scram. At the same time, Heydog would crank out his loudest 'ArRoooo' as many times as necessary to distract the bees.

As much as Kendal appreciated Heydog's offer, he didn't think it right for Heydog to risk getting stung for him.

"Now, don't you fret over me," Heydog said. "I haven't found a bee yet that can do me much damage. I'm immune from their stings. I can absorb as many stings as they want to waste on me. Don't worry. Now, get going, Kendal. It's a long ways home."

Chapter Five

# Baking Business Bound

When Kendal departed earlier to attend baking school, Queen Zoey raised the security alert to yellow, the color indicating a significant risk from attack by killer bees. In addition to a killer bees' threat, a second incident alarmed Zoey. Last night a scrawny skunk showed up to break in. He wanted a free honey meal and he didn't intend to leave a *scent* behind. Only the quick action by the entrance guards chased him away.

Entrance guards did a bustling business all day, checking ID's as thousands of field bees popped in and out. Most worker bees had already arrived home, finished for the day. But the guards kept their eyes open for Greeney. Kendal showed up first. He heard a meek voice call, "Kendal. Hi there. I'm over here in a notch. Am I cleared to come inside with you?"

Grateful Greeney showed up for work. Kendal led her indoors. The colony was placed on notice to treat the caterpillar as a special guest. She was given a free pass to roam, but to tread carefully. If one tower toppled, others surely would flop over causing a domino effect.

24

On entering the hive, Greeney stopped dead in her tracks. The size of the hive surprised her, so huge—the interior truly impressive. Having guessed how honey bees lived, Greeney saw for herself how bees lived in harmony.

Without disputing Greeney, Kendal presented her with the facts. Worker bees did become agitated. If confined indoors too long, they turned jittery. Or if they spent too much time dwelling on the drones' laziness, the worker bees turned angry. After all, the worker bees worked hard all day, sometimes working two jobs.

Kendal conducted the tour. Greeney followed, goggle eyed over the vastness of the main room. Dozens of towers reached to the ceiling, similar to a high rise apartment complex.

Not far from the entrance, Kendal stopped at a large brooding area. "Greeney … here, take a look … in this cell," Kendal said, mindful not to disturb the larva inside. "See that larva stretching," Kendal said. "She's getting ready to spin a cocoon to complete her development." He found it hard to believe in fifteen to twenty days, a transformed creature emerged as an adult bee, ready to go to work.

Under a hypnotic spell, Greeney gawked at the larva as it began to spin its cocoon. In a matter of days, Greeney must spin one too. She knew it was a process called metamorphosis that turned a caterpillar into a butterfly. She didn't want to think about metamorphosis. Ugh! Ugh!—bound by silky strings, made her doubly apprehensive. Kendal called her three times before he broke her trance.

"Greeney, when you're ready, we have to inspect the bakery," Kendal reminded her.

"Oh sure, Kendal," Greeney answered. I'm ready."—but hardly ready. She stood there motionless, preoccupied. She tried to gauge how long it might take to weave a cocoon large enough to fit her body.

As Kendal and Greeney descended in the dark, a doorway

lighted by fire flies led them forward. Kendal proceeded toward the bakery with Greeney at his heels.

A large room housed the unused bakery—dusty and messy, wherever Kendal stared. *There's lots of work here before I can start a bakery operation,* he thought. Kendal took inventory of the equipment. He sensed something was missing.

Greeney identified the missing equipment needed to set up a bakery ... a delivery cart and a mixing machine. Little did Greeney know she was the answer to both problems.

Kendal suggested instead of a delivery cart, that he fashion a cloth blanket stitched with a hundred pockets, a saddle bag look. With it draped over Greeney's back, she could make deliveries through the hive. Greeney agreed, if Kendal didn't overload her.

Kendal noticed a split bamboo rod, large enough for a caterpillar's body. With Greeney sloshing through the batter, a mixing machine was not needed. By running in place, she'd get her exercise too.

"You're not kidding, Kendal, are you?" she asked. "Let me see if I fit."

Greeney positioned herself comfortably in the half rod and ran in place. She thought she was running on a treadmill. "This works fine," she said.

No bakery ever succeeded without a sign. Kendal considered the many possibilities. Greeney suggested they name the bakery, 'Kendal's Kitchen.' She made a sign, posting it outside the door. As he admired Greeney's handiwork, Kendal realized she possessed creative talents. Perhaps, she might think of some way to sort through Mrs. Bright's financial problems.

If Kendal didn't waste time, finding 500 pounds of honey was possible. Actually, Mrs. Bright's problem affected more than her family. It involved Zoey and the retired queens. Both of their hives were in jeopardy if Aidan's mom sold the property on which the hives stood. *Not much time left before 10:00 a.m. the day after tomorrow,* Kendal thought.

"Hello, in there," boomed Tee's brash voice from the hallway.

"Hello," Kendal responded. "Come right in, whoever you are."

In bounced Tee on his rear legs, a mad scowl on his face. He stood there ready to pounce on the baking crew of two.

"I'm here to find the niche you suggested each drone must discover for himself," Tee said, in an argumentative tone. Tee intended to squeal to Queen Zoey, how Kendal dared make friends with the son of a beekeeper. Tee knew beekeepers took honey from their hives without asking the bees' permission. He figured he'd give Kendal advance warning as a courtesy. *After all,* Tee thought, *they were brother drones.*

"What's the problem, Tee?" asked Kendal. "What did I do to rile you up? After all, you tripped me in the hallway."

Provoked, Tee responded that Aidan's family might return to steal Zoey's honey and take it away. Tee guessed the Queen might reward him with a job, if he warned her of an imminent threat to the honey supply.

Greeney observed Tee's body language, how he shifted from the right legs, to the left legs and back again. Tee stuttered when he got nervous.

"C'mon, what's really eating you, Tee?" Greeney asked.

"I heard bees must watch out for big people who linger near their hives," insisted Tee.

"Tee, it's not size that counts," Kendal countered. "It's the head and heart that count."

"Well," Tee said. "I use my head and I don't see much heart in this hive. I can't get work."

"Greeney and I plan to launch a bakery operation. I can use some help,"

"Doing what?" Tee asked.

Kendal spieled off fifty things to do including: gathering ingredients and utensils, mixing batter, baking cakes, muffins and bread, decorating some products and delivering the goods. With so much to do, Kendal need an efficient staff of assistants.

Tee cracked a joint in his leg in excitement. "I'm in, if you want me," he said.

"You're hired," Kendal fired back. As equals, the crew of three plunged into work. With breakfast only ten hours away, they experimented by using a simple honey cake recipe to test their talents. Kendal's apprenticeship under Martha proved invaluable as he taught Greeney and Tee the bakery business. For no reason, Tee stopped working; he shuffled his feet and asked Kendal about hiring other drones. "Can't you use my friends, Kendal?"

"Oh, there's plenty of work to do," Kendal said. "See if you can round them up. Ask them to stop by tomorrow for an interview."

# Chapter Six

# A Growing Concern

Four bulky sized drones hovered outside the bakery, hanging onto every word uttered by Kendal and Tee. They decided they might not get another opportunity. In they hustled with heads held high. In unison they announced, "We're ready to go to work, boss."

Kendal stared at the four anxious drones. Under normal circumstances, drones never showed any enthusiasm over anything happening in the hive. *Why hire these guys?* He thought. *Were they qualified? Am I prepared to add more staff?* Kendal needed answers to these questions before he responded to the four job seekers.

Tee spoke in behalf of his friends. They were good guys. They belonged to an elite club known as the Gripers Gang. Not a day went by that they didn't gather to complain; they complained about everything. *Yipes!* Kendal thought. *Exactly what I need, grumpy additions to a stable work crew.*

"They're the best, Kendal. Each one has exceptional talents. Can't you let them try out for your team, Kendal? You know … give them the benefit of a doubt."

"Well, guys, I understand why you want to work. Give me a good reason to hire you."

Jockie introduced himself. His interests focused on sports and competition. He boasted that he worked out twice a day. The heavy work in a bakery suited him fine.

Bookie was the studious drone. He preferred learning over complaining. He thought his interests would prove useful in marketing the bakery products.

Mechie proudly called himself an inventor; on second thought, maybe more a mechanic. He fixed anything, even equipment not broken. Kendal needed his skills.

Handy was the silent drone; he never talked. Tee told Kendal that Handy needed coaching to get him involved; Tee had considered using a ventriloquist to talk for Handy. But Tee believed Handy was an invaluable worker in a production operation.

Kendal evaluated the talents and interests of the four drones.

"Let's give it a try, gang," Kendal said. "You're all hired. But remember who's in charge. Tee's your supervisor."

With the drones gathered around, Kendal provided a short orientation. He tried to teach them the techniques he learned from Queen Martha. Three times, Kendal repeated the main rule … always follow the recipe.

The Gripers Gang was game to get started. At first, the drones heeded Martha's advice. But soon they began to fuss over this and that, whether to add an ingredient or how long to leave the cakes bake, or, or … one or, after the other. Old habits were hard to break for grouchy complainers. After bickering for fifteen minutes, Tee whistled for attention. "Cut it out, guys."

As the batter thickened, Greeney stopped jogging. Tee poured batter into molds. Using the conveyor belt, the batter was moved into the oven. Tee assured Kendal he personally oiled the apparatus.

Bookie screamed. His hind legs were caught in the conveyor

belt. Kendal grabbed a cookie sheet pan and lodged it in the moving belt. Only Kendal's quick reflexes saved Bookie from roasting in the oven.

Handy didn't say boo, but he worked tirelessly. When Bookie screamed, Handy's toupee fell on the floor. Embarrassed, without a sound Handy picked up the toupee and reset it on his head. Kendal saw what happened but made no comment.

"Thanks for your kindness, Kendal." Handy's few words stunned everyone; they were the first words ever heard by the gripers. They were speechless.

One task remained ... Kendal decided to bake the first batch of miracle cakes for an early morning delivery. Kendal read the instructions to his crew, three times.

Kendal hummed as they worked. One after another, the whole crew joined in producing a melody of hums, high hums, low hums ... no ho hums. Mechie improvised as he rigged a sounding board of pans to amplify the sound. The music carried beyond the walls of the bakery.

The humming sound even carried outside the hive. There, the spider Spero stopped repairing a web as the monotonous sounds disturbed his concentration. He decided to seek out the source of the noise.

Creeping inside the hive, Spero surveyed the scene. Sure enough, the bees snored. He grappled up the inside wall to reach the ceiling. From there, Spero surveyed the colony ... forty thousand bees, all sound asleep. The humming came from another level beneath the floor of the main room.

As a bungee jumper stepping off a cliff, Spero launched himself in a free fall, releasing silk thread behind him. Not far above the floor, he braked in mid-air. With the silk thread holding him tight, Spero swung from side to side. He surveyed the sleepers to make sure they didn't stir.

One worker bee heard a sound; she rousted co-workers to investigate the noise. Maybe a prowler entered the hive. Spero knew trouble was coming. He let go of the thread, dropped to the floor, and scurried for the nearest exit. It led to the bakery and the drones.

"What's going on upstairs?" Tee yelled. "There's quite a commotion up there." Greeney glanced at the door and saw Spero creep through. She called out a warning to Kendal and the drones that a spider was sneaking into the bakery.

"What are you doing, spider?" Greeney asked. "Are you causing trouble again?"

Spero saw his predicament. He was outmanned and surrounded by six drones and Greeney, leaving him little choice. Upstairs, stinging bees stood between him and safety of his web. Impossible to try that route.

"I apologize," Spero tried to make amends to appease the drones.

Kendal's crew discussed their options. They decided Kendal was the right one to escort Spero out of the hive. With his white baker's hat as a flag of truce, Kendal might lead Spero outside safely.

As Kendal led Spero through the rows of agitated bees, the worker bees jeered at the spider; some pointed their stingers at him. "Don't you ever come back," one worker screamed.

As Spero prepared to scoot free, he asked Kendal why he treated a spider with such kindness. "Please tell me, strictly between a spider and a bee. ... Why?"

Kendal answered, "From the day I was hatched, I pledged always to act with kindness and help anyone in need, that's why."

"I'll find some way to thank you, Kendal." And Spero disappeared into the night.

When Kendal returned, the drones were at work. Mechie even designed a backup saddle bag for Greeney to make trips to the bakery for refills. The blanket with pockets was mounted on four sticks, typically used to support a pup tent. When Greeney bumped the sticks, the bag naturally would fall on her back.

Tired to the bone, Kendal called his crew together for a ceremony. He gave each drone a white fluffy baker's hat. He tried to place his last hat on Greeney's head—bad fit. He promised her to locate one to fit her odd shaped head.

Kendal thanked the team for their resourcefulness. They all deserved a long sleep to recover from a hectic day. He postponed taking a rest. He must stay awake to devise a plan to help Mrs. Bright. Time was short. Mrs. Bright had an appointment to discuss sale of her land that even affected both bee hives located on the land. With so many challenges facing him, Kendal anticipated a long night ahead of him.

# Chapter Seven

# Making A
# Case For Extra Honey

Szzzz … szzzz , steady streams of snoring almost knocked Rebecca over as she opened the bakery door. She never expected to find baker bees sprawled all over the room … Kendal dozed on the conveyor belt … Handy flopped on a stool … Greeney sprawled in the half bamboo rod with Tee draped over the edge … the others slumbered on top of tables. Rebecca maneuvered around the sleeping drones and tapped Kendal on the shoulder. As he stirred, Rebecca whispered that Queen Zoey wished him to join her for breakfast.

Quietly, Kendal and Rebecca slipped out of the bakery. When Kendal glanced into the Queen's chamber, he was thrilled by what he saw. All kinds of baked goods covered the table. Evidently, Tee and Greeney had made an early morning delivery while Kendal slept.

Tee and Greeney had knocked on the Queen's door before sunrise. Zoey invited them to come in. She tasted the blueberry muffin first. It became her favorite. She was disappointed to find only one in Greeney's blanket of pockets. She didn't know the blueberry mix contained the ingredients for miracle cakes. Kendal had issued instructions to ration the blueberry muffins until each bee received at least one.

And so as Kendal walked in, Zoey was preparing to enjoy her second breakfast. As she dropped a half eaten piece of cake on the floor, she sensed company behind her.

"Ah, good morning, Kendal. You didn't come see me last evening."

Kendal apologized. Not coming to see her was an oversight. When he arrived home, Greeney showed up to start work. They toured the hive and used all their energies to begin bakery operations. Tee then came along with his four drone friends. Hiring took more of his time. Zoey realized Kendal had a packed schedule.

Zoey told Kendal how impressed she was with his new first assistant. Tee definitely showed her he was a thinker; he demonstrated good business sense and he was a natural actor. She complimented Kendal for his selection of Tee.

The half-piece of cake lying on the floor caught Kendal's attention. He picked it up and tasted the product to check for quality. It tasted scrumptious. No burnt flavor. He swallowed a bite and asked Zoey how her day went yesterday. Reluctantly, Zoey admitted the day turned out as a down day for her. She laid only 1400 eggs. "Did I count right?" she asked Rebecca.

"Right on target, my queen," Rebecca said.

Her egg production count bothered Queen Zoey. Soon she must announce her retirement. Only this morning she discovered more whiskers on her chin. The bristles embarrassed her so much she asked Kendal if he noticed the black shoots. With diplomacy, he answered he didn't see as much facial growth as he noticed on other bees he met.

Kendal's answer gave Queen Zoey reason to crack a smile. She pictured Kendal's surprise when he encountered her sister queens, wearing long beards. Of course, Queen Victoria's beard was the most unique of all. In another six hundred years, it would grow longer than Greeney the caterpillar.

The conversation turned to Kendal's visit at the retirees' hive. Kendal described Victoria's hive fortress, Martha's baking techniques, how he earned his baker bee certificate and last, meeting with the Queens' Council. What pleased Kendal most, was the trust the Council placed in him. He almost keeled over when the Council shared its prized treasure—the recipe for miracle cakes.

Kendal moved on to describe his visit to Aidan's house. How he learned about Mrs. Bright's money problems from a friendly canary and by overhearing a private phone conversation. Aidan's mom revealed the families financial problems with a tight time table to resolve them. *Why the rush?* Queen Zoey wondered. Kendal explained how Mrs. Bright might be forced to sell the property on which the retirement hive and Queen Zoey's hive stood.

"Shoot, are you sure, Kendal?" Zoey asked as she stopped eating muffins to catch her breath. *The old oak tree—under the ax!* Zoey panicked. Rebecca screamed. She pictured the retirees becoming homeless bearded queen bees.

Zoey wasn't so upset about her family; they were young enough to swarm to a new hive. But the queen bees were too old to be relocated.

Kendal devised a plan to make them all secure. He intended to find 500 pounds of honey, somehow. That's the amount Mrs. Bright needed to pay her bills. If Kendal's plan had a chance to succeed, Zoey wanted to help. "I can spare 30 pounds out of our surplus," Zoey said. "That's subject, of course, to a consultation with the entire colony."

"I understand, Mother."

Rebecca subtracted 30 from 500 in her head. Her math worked without a calculator. The remainder was 470 pounds. It sounded impossible. Rebecca credited Kendal for his determination, but 470 pounds—no way.

"Rebecca, I heard Victoria say the queens have a surplus, much larger than 470 pounds," Kendal said. "I'll try to convince the Council to contribute the entire 470."

"Good luck," Rebecca said.

"Even if you succeed, Kendal," Zoey said, "won't the family end up in the same predicament when it sells 500 pounds?"

Kendal admitted his mother's concern was a valid one. For that reason, he left six sample miracle cakes on Aidan's table. Mrs. Bright with her experience as a beekeeper naturally would be curious about the nuggets. She'd have them analyzed. With the formula for miracle cakes in hand, the family was assured of steady income for a very long time.

*Kendal's plan might just work,* Zoey thought. She encouraged Kendal to try to convince the 303 queens. They might be willing to donate to such a good cause. Zoey scratched out a note for Kendal to take to Queen Leah.

"Bring this note to your grandmother, Kendal. I'm asking Queen Leah to support you as you argue your case before the Council. She's only one vote, but every vote counts."

Before Kendal departed, Queen Zoey promised to deliver her 30 pounds of honey to ground level by the next morning. A mound of that much honey next to a tree would be an eye catcher,

"That's wonderful, Mother," Kendal said. "I'll tell the drones what you're doing. One of them might see Aidan playing with Heydog. Once Heydog learns that honey will be deposited on the ground, he can watch for it and signal Aidan's family."

Rebecca checked the time. "We'd better be on the way to your briefing of the colony, your highness." Rebecca knew the worker bees became agitated by late briefings that changed their routines.

Queen Zoey lumbered down the hallway with Kendal at her side. Rebecca tagged along behind. She overheard snatches of the conversation as Zoey and her son chatted all the way. She picked up a few words … longevity … royalty … confidence … getting tired ... retirement. By piecing together these few words, the meaning became clear to Rebecca.

The entire colony was assembled, waiting for the Queen. Moving to the podium, Zoey spoke. "Good morning, my family. I promise not to take long. I know you're anxious to go to work." Zoey's opening remark spurred on a loud buzz from the assembly.

A female worker in the back row asked to speak. The queen agreed.

"When I flew through the fields yesterday, my Queen, I noticed Kendal sailing through the air in a mad hurry. Since this isn't mating season, what prompted him to fly so fast?"

Zoey gave Kendal the opportunity to explain what happened. Members of the audience knew Kendal's name. Many worker bees saw his name posted on a sign outside the bakery. Others heard his name mentioned by drones as they served cakes and muffins in the cafeteria. Kendal's name came up as stories were repeated about his acts of kindness.

As Kendal positioned himself next to Queen Zoey, he stared into forty thousand faces. The sight humbled him; he was new at public speaking.

"My sisters and brothers. My life has not been dull the past few days." Kendal recounted how Queen Zoey allowed him to study baking and set up the bakery shop. He proceeded to tell the assembly about the special secret recipe, Queen Martha gave him. The miracle cakes would keep them healthy and safe from pestering mites aiming to eat out their bodies. Starting today, he reported, medicinal cakes were being added to their daily diet. A few of the cakes were distributed as blueberry muffins this morning. Queen Zoey licked her lips repeatedly. No wonder the muffin tasted so good.

Cheers boomed from the audience, bouncing off the walls. The adult bees knew what kind of devastation mites caused in hives, even death for baby bees.

Kendal waited until the noise died down. He told the assembly about his visit to Aidan, the boy they all saw dashing through the forest talking to animals and insects. He finished by explaining how much Aidan's family needed help or face losing their home to the bank.

Kendal reminded his audience that honey bees earned a reputation for their generosity to people, going back thousands of years. What other creatures have fed people as bees have done so generously? He asked for their good will now, to give Aidan's family similar treatment. He turned to Queen Zoey to make the plea for help.

Queen Zoey addressed all her children telling them she'd like to contribute 30 pounds of surplus honey to help Aidan's family. If anyone objected, the time was right to express it … Hearing no complaints or questions, she proceeded to close the briefing with a parental warning. If any worker bee saw strangers today, she should report it to Rebecca. For their safety, she ordered a doubling of the guards at the entrance in the event killer bees attempted a forced entry.

As Zoey finished her briefing, the large doors leading from the basement opened wide. In marched five drones with Tee leading; they pushed heavily loaded carts. Everyone dressed smartly in their baker bee white fluffy hats. Behind them, Greeney labored under the weight of her saddle blanket with tasty treats spilling over the brims of a hundred pockets.

The drones passed the cakes and muffins with worker bees pitching in to help. Would wonders never cease? Female worker bees were assisting drones. Greeney kept busy; she made three trips to the bakery for refills. When snack time was over, the colony thundered its appreciation. Kendal beamed with delight.

For dramatic effect, Greeney hastily shed her saddle blanket. Encouraged by the bees' applause, she performed a caterpillar dance. Greeney rose up on her ten hind legs … her head and chest swinging from side to side. She rocked in hip hop fashion.

Next she flung her six front legs in every imaginable way … waving, flexing, bending and sweeping … with a grace and a beat never seen before. The onlookers gaped at her antics. Her rear legs propelled her body forward, slow steady steps going forward, sidewards, and backwards, doing a delayed dead stop, only to resume again. Not one bee was able to imitate Greeney's complicated caterpillar dance.

Impressed by Greeney's performance, Rebecca gave it a try. She only knew a wiggle waggle, a six step dance, familiar to all worker bees. They performed that same dance to point out the direction other worker bees should take to find the tastiest nectar.

As the dancing spectacle ended, the worker bees said goodbye as they flew to their jobs. The drones and Greeney returned to the bakery. Queen Zoey asked Kendal, Rebecca and Tee to remain for a chat.

The Queen confided in them. She had just made one of the hardest decisions in her life. Never before had she enlisted a spy. But Zoey must send someone into killer bee territory to learn the enemy's war plans.

"Tee, will you play spy for me? It's a critical mission," Zoey asked.

Both Tee and Kendal were floored to hear the Queen's request. Drones received no training to be secret agents. Tee was concerned what the colony might think of him. If he changed sides to join the killer bees' army, he'd be marked as a traitor.

Zoey explained she picked Tee because of his intelligence, enthusiasm and his acting talent. If anyone was capable to bluff the enemy, the Queen thought Tee fit the bill. If Tee agreed, the Queen intended to announce he deserted only after he departed to join the enemy.

The Queen noticed Kendal's discomfort and asked, "Kendal, what do you think about my idea to send Tee into harm's way?"

"If it were me," Kendal replied, "reluctantly, I'd accept the appointment to save the colony." He said he had one hundred percent confidence in Tee to do the job but—with Kendal's vote of confidence, Tee said he'd try to infiltrate the killer bees' colony.

Minutes later, Kendal and Tee silently made their way toward the entrance; each one had a special mission. Kendal reassured Tee the colony eventually would learn of his sacrifice to protect the whole family.

"Be off and good acting, my friend," Kendal said to Tee as he slapped him on the back. As an afterthought, Kendal suggested Tee take his baker's hat with him in the event the enemy asked about his occupation. The fluffy white hat proved Tee earned a certificate as a full-fledged baker bee. Kendal guessed the enemy might be suspicious to hear that any drone performed kitchen duty.

"You be careful, my friend," Kendal told Tee as they parted. They ascended going in separate directions.

## Chapter Eight

# Yoodle's Yoke

Nine miles to the south of Queen Zoey's hive, the killer bees scampered through their hive in typical turmoil. Their confusion traced directly to Queen Yoodle's leadership. She dominated them. Whatever her bees did or didn't do, were regulated by three volumes of Yoodle's rules. If anyone broke a rule, the punishment followed automatically.

Killer worker bees competed with each other to come up with the most descriptive names to call Yoodle. She didn't care. The more Yoodle was criticized, it gave her ammunition to indulge in her favorite hobby ... to punish or kill either family or foe. So what if the bees called her wacky or miserable, who cared? So what if the bees found her repulsive and smelly, who dared tell her? "Show no mercy" was her famous motto. She proposed to conquer all hives to the north as her mission in life.

The killer bees followed frequent flying orders from Queen Yoodle to swarm north. Heading south was not an option for them. Not even killer bee colonies remaining down south permitted Yoodle's renegades to come their way.

In the sub basement, a handful of Yoodle's subjects secretly were plotting against her. Three conspirators were whispering. One guy bellyached … Yoodle's hive was nothing but a big mess … the honey combs were falling apart … bodies were piling up faster than the embalmers disposed of them … the honey turned to tasteless goo … and the baby bees were uncared for.

The second drone agreed. Recently, he heard that workers were spreading a rumor the colony was preparing to swarm real soon.

"No way," the third drone complained. "That's eight times this year."

Without pausing for a breath, the first drone added his two cents worth. "If we don't steal other bees' honey—we'll starve."

A noise startled the three drones. The heavy door flew open behind them. Two lieutenants glared at the drones with a menacing stare. "We heard you guys. We'll stop your complaints." The lieutenants slammed the door. The drones were sealed in their tomb as the door was bolted behind them.

Proudly, the two lieutenants marched up the stairs. They belonged to an elite group of 100 lieutenants. All were expert killers.

At the hive entrance, Queen Yoodle counted heads as worker bees returned from the fields. Each worker saluted the Queen. The proper way to salute was covered by rule eighteen of Yoodle's three volumes of Rules.

Yoodle screamed, using a megaphone, "Where are my scouts? Where are those two lazy louts I sent out to search for hives in the north?"

No one risked answering for fear of being punished. Only a crazy bee dared to answer Yoodle when she exploded in her foul frame of mind. As Yoodle tired of counting heads, she turned on her heels—time for her nap.

An alarm sounded. It shattered the silence demanded by the queen of all her subjects.

Half of the colony poured out of the hive. A scrawny skunk,

earlier chased from Queen Zoey's hive, tried to break into Yoodle's hive. One mistake didn't prevent him from a second stupid attempt.

Soon the skunk turned into a pin cushion. Stingers covered his body. The poor thing died as he tried to escape. For a whole hour, the killer bees persisted to buzz about in a rage. Whenever they started to settle down, lieutenants whipped them up again.

In all the confusion, a stranger joined the ranks of the angry killers. At the entrance, a security check detained the drone. When the guards recognized a stranger's scent, they arrested him.

"Hold on, you. Stand still. Wings up. Who are you?" the head guard demanded.

"My name is Tee," he replied. "I have information for your queen about your missing scout."

"All right, Tee. Follow me. I'll take you to our leader."

The head guard decided to escort Tee to Queen Yoodle. Two other guards followed closely, ready to sting Tee if he did anything suspicious.

Queen Yoodle awakened. She stood by her bed, enthralled by the reflection in her mirror. *Not bad at all,* she thought. *Beauty is not in the eye of the beholder. It's right here in my mirror.* A knock on the door interrupted her pleasure.

"Queen Yoodle," the head guard called. "We arrested a stranger at the entrance."

"What's the matter with you? Don't you know I'm busy?" she replied curtly.

"But a drone says he has information about a scout, Your Highness."

"Drones are no good, any of them … " Yoodle screamed. "Bring him in. Let's hear what words of wisdom an ignorant drone has to offer me."

She beckoned Tee to come forward, but not too close. Tee shied away, as far away as possible. The odor from Yoodle's body was stronger than Greeney's disgusting bad breath.

"Who are you?" Yoodle demanded without making eye contact.

"My name is Tee. I live in Zoey's hive where one of your scouts tried to infiltrate."

Yoodle lost patience. She commanded Tee to hurry up. Her time was precious, not to be wasted. So Tee told her the scout was executed, as far as he knew. That infuriated Yoodle to think two scouts she sent out might have been caught. "That's hogwash!" she exclaimed.

"But, Queen Yoodle,"—the head guard interrupted.

"Silence," she retorted. "How dare you speak without my permission?"

"Oops, sorry about that, Your Highest," she answered in panic. She was careful to say Your Highest. Yoodle forbade the use of Your Highness, a civilized expression.

"Keep your mouth shut till I tell you to open it."

Yoodle questioned the reliability of Tee's information. When Tee told her he was a baker bee, she dropped her chin, weighed down by doubt. She wanted proof. Tee reached into his pouch for his fluffy white hat and put it on his head. "See … Your Highness, the mark of my trade."

"Tee, I'll say this only once. When you address me, you will call me Your Highest, if you know what's good for you. I like eating healthy food. I'll give you a trial as my baker."

Tee felt reassured; he had successfully penetrated the queen's inner circle of killer bees. She believed his story. If only he kept his cool. Now he must take the next step. Tee admitted he knew the location of Zoey's hive.

She only smirked. "Of course you know where you live. Do you think I'm stupid?"

Tee held his temper. What a temptation for him to be sarcastic but—he acted mum as an Egyptian mummy wrapped tightly.

Queen Yoodle decided to teach Tee a lesson or two. "Lock up this drone," she commanded.

Yoodle then issued her order for all lieutenants to report immediately. Blindly, they obeyed. As the lieutenants entered the meeting hall, each one bowed. They knew rule eighteen of Yoodle's three volumes of Rules required a proper salute.

One lieutenant bristled over being insulted by another. She stung the second lieutenant, both of them died, mortally wounded after losing their stingers. Yoodle ordered their bodies carted away. The Queen always replaced lieutenants from her list of chosen candidates. Recruits were drafted; they had no choice.

As one lieutenant showed up late, Queen Yoodle screamed in her familiar shrill voice. "Toss her into the dungeon overnight. Let's see if Tee enjoys confinement with one of my nasty ladies. Take this lieutenant away, now."

After Tee was dumped into a dingy dungeon by the guards, he started to plan his next move. As he paced, he became sick to his stomach. The stench proved unbearable after a minute in the cell. He shivered with the biting damp cold. Tee was certain the attack on Zoey's hive was planned. He had to worm his way into Yoodle's confidence to learn her plans.

The dungeon door banged open. Two guards tossed in the struggling lieutenant.

"You have company," one of the guards announced. "Aren't you the lucky one? I hope you're still alive in the morning."

Tee rushed to the lieutenant's aid. Tenderly, he helped her to her feet. He thought it was unfair to throw a lieutenant into jail. After all, rank deserved some respect and privileges.

The lieutenant, named Louisi, assured him rank meant zero in Queen Yoodle's army. Tee fascinated her. A drone never acted kindly to any worker bee she knew. Louisi asked Tee who he was. With his chin out, Tee declared he graduated as a baker bee. He was assigned to an important mission.

"Well, we're stuck together for the night," Louisi commented. "What's your name?"

"It's Tee."

"You mean the letter, 't,' nothing more than that?" Louisi asked.

"No … T-E-E."

Fortunately, Tee had stocked his pockets with baked honey cakes. He asked Louisi if she were hungry. Louisi rubbed around her stomach; hunger pains gnawed at her insides. So the two prisoners sat down to enjoy the goodies.

Learning that Tee was a baker bee tickled Louisi. She asked Tee where he learned to bake. Happily, he told Louisi about a drone named Kendal who taught drones the bakers' trade. His friend Kendal was the kindest bee anywhere. In fact, Kendal was a real prince.

For some reason, Tee felt comfortable speaking with Louisi. He told her about Kendal's mission to help a young boy and his family with money problems. Kendal hoped to distribute a recipe for miracle cakes for the benefit of bees throughout the world.

"Tee, you describe this Kendal as a crusader," Louisi remarked. "He's certainly a generous drone. I'll confide in you, Tee. In Queen Yoodle's hive, you won't find any kindness. I really shouldn't be telling you this stuff. It means a death sentence for me."

"Don't fear, Louisi. My lips are sealed. Is it that bad in your hive?"

"My Queen is a scoundrel. Some day I'll shake loose from her clutches. I don't know when or how, but I will."

"Tell me, Louisi, what do the other lieutenants think about Queen Yoodle?" Knowing the hive's sentiments about their Queen might help Zoey in her planning.

Louisi confided in Tee that there were two lieutenants who agreed with her views. They were ready to join a revolt at the right time.

As Tee and Louisi talked, they shared thoughts and hopes for a brighter future. Because the dungeon was damp and cold, Louisi snuggled against Tee's side. Eventually they fell asleep.

At the crack of dawn, Louisi was released. As a guard unlatched the door, she cuffed her squarely on the chin to teach the guard never to mishandle a lieutenant again.

Sitting in the dungeon alone, it dawned on Tee that being alone and far from home caused a terrible strain. But thanks to Kendal, he had a chance to make his mark in life. He had proved himself as a clever baker bee and a now as a secret agent. As he folded his legs tightly against his body, the shivering became bearable. Tee waited to be summoned. At least, he hoped to be sent for soon.

# Chapter Nine

# A Weighty Decision

With Tee away playing spy, Kendal was playing his numbers game … 303 was an interesting number. 303 strong willed, independent queens needed convincing to share their wealth. Their honey surplus held the key to Mrs. Bright's problems. But Kendal only had a few minutes left to make his case before the Queens' Council.

Guarding the retirees' hive entrance, Mame and Dame were working out … doing push ups and leg bends, and lifting weights. Both of the brawny queens preferred to earn respect for their brains, not only for their generous physiques. For the present they must be content with body building.

A sweaty workout didn't prevent the wrestlers from talking, even debating each other. That's exactly what the queens were doing behind the Council's closed doors.

"Dame, how do you rate Kendal?" Mame asked.

"At the … the top of any … any bees' … scale," Dame sputtered as she completed a hundred pushups. Kendal has proved himself to be competitive, a sure winner. Mame and Dame agreed that Kendal deserved a champion's ring.

"Shhhh ... somebody's coming," Dame whispered. "It's our champion—"

"Hello, Queen Dame. Hello, Queen Mame."

"Good morning, Kendal," they responded. He was making rounds as a roving ambassador. He was here ... gone ... and here again.

Kendal came to seek an audience with the Council. He shared the Bright's money problems with Mame and Dame. They promised their support, their two votes. With Leah's vote, that made three. Only three hundred votes to win.

Kendal worried about the mood of the queens this morning. Mame spoke bluntly; the queens were feisty. Queen Leah skipped through the hallway. She possessed great instincts for knowing when someone new arrived at the hive. Leah called, "Hello, hello, my dear boy. I'm so glad you came to visit. What brings you back so soon?"

Kendal explained Aidan's family problems. The Brights needed 500 pounds of honey on short notice. He handed Leah his mother's note.

"Please read it to me, Kendal. I left my glasses at the beauty shop."

"Sure, Grandma." It reads:

*Dear Mother,*

*How are you? Kendal and I appreciate what you did to help Kendal earn his Baker Bee's certificate.*

*Your grandson follows a path of kind deeds. His attention is now directed at helping a local family in need. Unless Mrs. Bright can find money quickly, the family might lose its home. To pay the current bills, she needs 500 extra pounds of honey. I've offered 30 pounds from our limited inventory. Kendal comes today to petition the Queens' Council for the balance of 470 pounds of honey.*

*At first, I didn't believe it possible to accumulate so*

*much honey in a hive's stores. Kendal assures me your*
*surplus is even larger. Please support him as much as you*
*can when he appears before the decision makers.*
    *My appreciation and love.*
    *Your daughter, Zoey*

Queen Zoey's message touched Leah deeply. Urging Kendal to accompany her, they hurried to the Council chamber. A lively debate thundered through the closed doors. Leah coaxed the door open, preventing the hinges from squeaking. Queen Victoria stood at the podium. Exhausted, she struggled to maintain a semblance of order.

The air was hot, almost suffocating. Weary queens gathered in small groups like patches of wilting wild flowers. Each group argued its position as the right one.

"Please, ladies," insisted Queen Victoria. "This Council must come to order."

Bickering made it difficult for Victoria to maintain proper decorum. For the last two hours, the queens argued ... pro and con ... whether to establish a charm school in the basement near the beauty shop ... yes or no ... do it or don't do it ... is it needed or not?

Queen Victoria banged her gavel; enough's, enough. "Let's table the motion until we meet again," she ordered.

Consulting her agenda, Queen Victoria tried to see who entered the back door. Kendal stood waiting next to Queen Leah. A diversion was welcome. Queen Victoria peered at the newcomers. Using her own form of sign language, Leah indicated Kendal wished to address the Council. Queen Victoria caught on.

"Kendal, good morning," Victoria acknowledged. A grand silence followed as the queens interrupted their arguing.

Victoria waved to Kendal. "Come, join me. Tell us what's on your mind today."

Apprehensively, Kendal started up the aisle. He glanced left and right, smiling at each queen. What arguments could he use on the queens? That was the question bothering Kendal. He considered the various options to convince the Council to donate a large portion of its honey supply to strangers. He was at a loss. *Oh well,* he reminded himself, *I'll do my best and let their good judgment do the rest.*

At the podium, Kendal drew in a deep, *slooow* breath. He plunged into his speech.

"Your highness, Queen Victoria … Grandma Leah and ladies of the Council … I come to you with an urgent need." He described his relationship to Aidan and his family. They were in jeopardy of losing their home because of financial problems. Mrs. Bright didn't have enough money to pay all her bills. She might lose not only her home, but all her property, unless she found 500 pounds of honey to sell. Mrs. Bright couldn't ask any more of her own colonies. They were producing at one hundred percent of capacity.

Kendal added that Queen Zoey pledged 30 pounds of her surplus to help. In the spirit of giving, he appeared before this Council to plead for its help.

"I come to you with hat in hand."—For dramatic effect, Kendal placed the white fluffy hat on his head—"to ask you to contribute 470 pounds of honey to help Aidan's family."

Kendal's request cooled the air. Reactions were mixed. A weathered worn old queen in the back of the room moaned. A few queens rustled their wings; a few shook their heads in disbelief; still another opposed the proposition. Most of the queens just concentrated on Kendal's words. The old queen, who moaned, cried. At ninety years old, she lived through the days of economic depression. She knew what it meant to go hungry.

A perky queen, with a lapel pin reading number 200, asked why Aidan's family problem became their responsibility. Kendal answered with honesty. "Of course, Aidan's family isn't your responsibility. Aidan's mother has one option left. She can sell the land on which the old oak tree stands."

The deadline for decision loomed. At 10:00 o'clock sharp the next morning, Mrs. Bright was scheduled to meet with her agent, right in front of the old oak tree. They were to discuss sale of the land around the old oak tree to lumber companies.

Number 200 grasped the significance. "Mrs. Bright might sell our property; our tree might be cut down," she declared.

"I'm afraid number 200 is on target, Queen Victoria," Kendal said. "Mrs. Bright is at her wits end. She loves this oak tree. It's her favorite among the thousands growing on her property."

After only one hour, debate ended. Queen Martha spoke up. "I favor contributing the 470 pounds of honey. It's only part of our surplus. All we're doing is what bees have been doing for millions of years, sharing honey with people. The Brights are an outstanding family in our community. They need help."

Queen Martha hoped Kendal's contact with Mrs. Bright might pave the way to spread the recipe for miracle cakes throughout the bee world.

Kendal was one step ahead of Martha. That was the reason he left six miracle cakes on Aidan's kitchen table in full sight. Undoubtedly, Mrs. Bright would have the sample cakes analyzed. Scientists examining the ingredients would find they were capable of producing healthy benefits for bees.

Martha reminded the queens how their own surplus came from hard work of other bees. "Let's get real, my sisters," Queen Martha exhorted, "We should be willing to give back after accepting so much from others, even giving to perfect strangers."

The ninety year old queen, who was born in the depression, asked to be heard. "Even though I'm insecure, I offer a motion to contribute our 470 pounds of honey." The motion passed without dissent.

Kendal rocketed towards the ceiling, pumped up with joy. He landed back at the podium, still flapping his wings in applause. Kendal's actions set off a chain reaction; the others clapped too.

"Thank you a million times, my ladies," Kendal blurted out.

Queen Leah ran over to him. "Grandson," she said, "I'm so proud of you."

"And here's your hat," Queen Martha added. "You dropped it during the debate."

Time was short. The many preparations for honey collection required Kendal's attention. Neither of the two hives ever tried to give away honey before.

Queen Victoria assigned Mame and Dame to coordinate the honey delivery outdoors.

They appreciated the opportunity to prove they had brain power. Mame took the lead. She thought their fortress layout offered many advantages ... a storehouse in the basement, the tunnels and the swinging exit door, used for honey deliveries. But, they needed a chute to slide the honey to the ground.

Dame did a somersault in excitement. "Good thinking, Mame." Then she called together twenty tag teams, every one with lots of muscle. These ladies were capable of easily lifting the honey cylinders and moving them to a drop off point. But lowering the cylinders to the ground was a major challenge. Martha volunteered to stitch a sturdy chute.

Dame asked Kendal for his reactions. "You two are priceless," Kendal said. "It's no wonder you win all your wrestling matches. My only suggestion is that you drop a little honey before 10:00 o'clock, to get the family's attention. Once they spot a pile of honey, that's when the fun begins."

"I think we're finished here," Kendal said. He prepared to leave when Queen Leah broke her silence, a grand slam proposal.

Chapter Ten

# Old Queens Fly Again

Leah had listened while her sisters presented their great ideas to help the Brights. A more novel idea popped into her head—

Sensing his grandmother wanted to speak, Kendal stared in her direction. She winked. He got the message; Leah began to speak. She offered what might seem to the others an outlandish proposition: "Let's double the honey appeal," she declared.

"How's that possible, Grandma?" Kendal asked in amazement. The others shook their heads in disbelief. What, a second 500 pounds of honey … that's impossible.

Leah outlined a united appeal plan. Her plan involved all of the hives in the vicinity. She was sure every hive between the old oak tree and Aidan's house knew the Bright family. Their care and concern for their bee colonies was well known. As a considerate beekeeper, Mrs. Bright deserved their help.

Queen Leah believed the local queen bees might approve a collection appeal. Without debate, the others agreed to pursue Queen Leah's suggestion. It might work. Queen Victoria, as the most experienced administrator, took charge. She always carried a set of prepared questions to develop an action plan ... *Who? What? When? Where? and How?*

*Who* is to be in charge? Leah volunteered to take the lead role.

*What* will they do? Leah proposed a collection drive involving all local colonies. The retirees to serve as solicitors.

*When* does the work begin? The answer was simple. Now. There were seven hours remaining before dusk to contact all the local queens.

*Where* does the solicitation take place? Queen Leah mapped out a territory between the old oak tree and Aidan's house. Only three years ago she used this same route the Bright family traveled coming to the old oak tree. If she remembered correctly, there were four hundred hives along the route.

*How* can all the requirements be completed on time? Queen Leah proposed asking for retirees to volunteer.

"My sisters ... Kendal," Leah asked, "Do you have any more questions before we adjourn?"

There were a few. Can the old queens fly after all their years in retirement? Are the retired queens able to find their way in the forest? Can the oldest queens with colonial Virginian accents be understood? Kendal proposed to recruit enough drones to escort the queens, even if he had to lean on other colonies for help.

Victoria insisted each queen must qualify to prove her ability to perform the duties of an active volunteer. Leah suggested a simple procedure to determine the fitness of each queen—line up the volunteers, conduct an eye test, weigh them, and test both their ability and agility to fly.

The wheels were spinning. Queens Martha, Mame and Dame hurried off to do their jobs in the collection drive. Kendal bid his farewell with a promise that drones would report to Queen Leah within two hours. Victoria and Leah ran off to locate as many volunteer queens as possible. After explaining her plan, Leah asked for a show of hands. Who was prepared to help?

Over a hundred volunteers were willing. The real question

was who was able?

Queen Leah knew the abilities of her sister queens: four were excused for poor eyesight, even with corrective lenses; thirteen were unable to work out the kinks in their wings and sixteen were overweight, not able to fly. One hundred retirees remained in the volunteer pool, both willing and able.

The remaining hundred queens were arranged in order by the numbers on their badges … the youngest assigned to travel the furthest, the oldest to contact hives closest to the old oak tree and the others to visit hives in between. Number 253 reminded Queen Leah that local queen bees don't take kindly to stranger queens invading their turfs. Typically, that's grounds for a battle royal.

"That's an excellent observation, number 253." Leah apologized for forgetting 253's name. "We'll let the escorting drone act as the advance man to make the initial contact at each hive." No one feared drones. Each one could approach under a flag of truce, using a white fluffy hat or some reasonable facsimile.

As Kendal promised, the contingent of drones reported to Victoria for escort duty. They were attired in black capes since none of them owned a tuxedo. One drone introduced himself as Handy, one of Kendal's assistants. It was his assignment as the supervisor of the operation. The pairing of drones with queens, moved speedily under Handy's supervision. Off they flew to their destinations. Victoria watched from the hive entrance, proud of the queens and the drones.

✳✳✳

Aidan was playing in the forest, with Heydog chasing him. Overhead, they heard the excited drones and piping queens. Aidan and Heydog stopped to watch.

A drone descended, landing on Heydog's head, behind his ear. "My name is Handy," the drone said. "Kendal won support for 500 pounds of honey for Aidan's mom. We're on the way to gather more honey from local hives. Look for deposits on the ground tomorrow, Heydog. I thought you should know." Handy pecked on Heydog's ear and flew off with the queen at his side.

By nightfall all of the retirees returned safely at the sides of their escorts. The drones were thanked and dismissed. Meeting in the Council chamber, the retirees relaxed; they were ready for bed.

Local queens, most of them, were receptive to a request for help. One exhausted queen admitted her visit reminded her of Halloween trick or treating. Another reported confronting one selfish queen who blatantly refused any help. A third queen ran into a problem when three angry worker bees decided to attack her drone escort. "Since my drone friend had no way to defend himself," she boasted, "I took charge and stung each one of them; we solved that problem."

Victoria and Leah thanked the exhausted volunteers. They performed beautifully. Tomorrow would show the fruits of their labor.

"Let's go to bed," Victoria suggested. "I'll see you all before 10:00 a.m."

Leah flipped off her thoughts about honey and about queens to concentrate on her grandson. Kendal, the poor boy, was over-burdened with so many problems. But far away, he was starting another project.

## Chapter Eleven

# Thirty Pounds

As Kendal hustled toward Zoey's hive, he broke out in a grin. He didn't believe his grandmother was so resourceful. Leah dreamt up a united way effort to double the honey collection; what an awesome idea. *Good genes,* he thought. Zoey surely inherited Leah's intelligence and charming ways. And Kendal stood next in line. So—

Kendal found Zoey in the brooding chamber. Her head hung down to her chest; he knew something was wrong.

"What's the problem, Mother?" he asked.

Zoey shared her concerns. "The guards arrested a second killer bee scout; she tried to sneak into the hive."

Zoey told Kendal the whole story. She met her responsibility for the colony by ordering the killer bee scout's imprisonment. Guards locked the enemy scout in the same jail cell with the first one whom they had apprehended the other day. Later, as the guards patrolled the hallway, they heard shouting, wailing, banging on the wall, a terrible commotion. They called it a cacophony.

"Kendal, do you know what the guards meant by cacophony?"

"Yes, Mother. Bookie used the word cacophony to describe the noise the drones made, when they washed pots and pans in the metal sink. Bookie said cacophony means harsh sounds."

Now Zoey understood. That's exactly what drew the guards' attention. By the time they opened the cell door, the guards found both bees on their backs with their legs kicking in the air.

"Are they all right, Mother?" Kendal inquired showing genuine concern.

"No, Kendal, they're both dead. They argued and fought; they stung each other fatally."

"Wow," Kendal reacted as he visualized the scene. "It sounds grisly."

Zoey admitted her day wasn't too great: two dead killer bees, Tee still in harm's way as her assigned spy, and a miserably low egg count. But Zoey was heartened to know she helped Aidan's family with a 30 pound donation of honey.

"How did you do with the Queens' Council?" she asked.

Grinning from antenna to antenna, Kendal reported that the Council approved the entire package of 470 pounds of honey. Only minimum debate; no one opposed.

Queen Zoey scampered over to Kendal to give him a big hug for doing the near impossible. She knew how stressful it was to switch the retirees' attention from a debate into action.

Kendal dropped his dilly of a surprise in Zoey's lap. Grandma Leah proposed a brand new idea. She convinced the queens to organize a voluntary effort to double honey collections. All local hives were being canvassed to participate. Handy accepted responsibility to organize the drones to act as escorts for queen volunteers.

"I'm not surprised, Kendal. Your grandmother was a planner in her time. The bakery in the basement was her idea … Please tell me how I can deliver on my pledge of 30 pounds by morning."

"The drones will help," Kendal reassured Zoey. "As soon as they return from escort service, we'll work out a delivery system. Not to worry."

When Kendal entered the bakery, he found Greeney working alone. The other bakery crew members were assigned to escort duty.

"How are you doing, Greeney? All that running in place has to be tiring."

"Not really, Kendal," she said, as she picked up her pace a bit. "I don't cover much ground, whether slithering through the grass or jogging in my bamboo rod.—Kendal, I need to talk."

"Sure, Greeney." Kendal anticipated bad news. On top of his other concerns, he didn't need another problem at this time. But Greeney held a special place in his heart. She was the same as family to him.

Halting in place, Greeney wiped batter splashed on her chin. She shared her fear of spinning her own cocoon. Her appetite for milkweed was growing every minute. Her time had come. With Kendal's permission, she intended to slip out this evening. She knew where milkweed was plentiful.

Kendal understood. But he also knew Greeney to be a tough act to follow.

Greeney carefully looked around the bakery. She admitted to mixed emotions about leaving. On one hand, metamorphosis was a necessary next step. On the other hand, she knew Kendal. He depended on her. If she found a replacement to mix the batter and transport the bakery products, that might solve both problems.

At Kendal's request, Greeney waited until dark. Some birds loved nothing more than a juicy caterpillar to carry back to their nest. She understood. A few weeks earlier, she had a narrow escape when two robins fought over her. In the confusion, she escaped by crawling into the notch of a tree trunk.

✳✳✳

With evening hovering over the horizon, both hives worked feverishly. In Zoey's hive, the drones located the wax capped honey cells. They pushed all the cylinders closer to the hive entrance.

Not far away, Mame and Dame organized their tag teams. They decided they needed a descriptive name. "We'll call ourselves the UBS," Mame suggested, as she caught the tag team members off guard.

"What's UBS stand for?" asked Dame without a clue.

"UBS stands for United Bee Service," answered Mame. "Does the name hit you, sisters?" They agreed the name had a familiar ring to it.

All twenty tag teams were assigned to gather honey capsules. They easily moved the cylinders to a drop off area. They pulled and they pushed, until the cylinders were properly arranged to be slid down the chute in the morning.

Meanwhile Greeney roamed outside, hunting for milkweed plants. Slowly, she descended the bark of the tree. With her nimble body, she squeezed through cracks and climbed over the crusted mounds of bark standing in her way. Going down proved more fun than climbing up. She licked her mouth as she edged downward. The thought of the sharp taste of milkweed occupied her attention.

*What's lurking there? A movement in the jagged cracks.* As Greeney moved closer, she recognized spindly legs. A large spider eased out into the open for his evening jaunt.

"Hello there," Greeney called. "Is that you, Spero? I can't see too well in the dark."

The spider hesitated answering. "You got it right, Greeney. I see you. It's safer out here than in the hive. How's my buddy Kendal doing?"

She explained how Kendal faced a terrible problem. By morning, the drones in the hive were scheduled to drop honey cylinders. Kendal worried about the long drop from the limb. He expected the cylinders to break on impact.

Spero agreed. He was a pro on dropping; that was his specialty, perfected by using his silky thread. He knew the safe way to fall.

As dark clouds passed in front of the moon, the night turned pitch-black. Spero asked Greeney her destination. She admitted a tasty meal brought her down the tree. She also had recruiting to do. She needed a caterpillar interested in learning a new occupation.

Spero was glad to help. A few minutes ago, he spied two caterpillars. They didn't seem busy. If Greeney followed him, Spero knew exactly where he last spotted the chewers.

Greeney explained how Kendal's plan provided honey for Aidan's family. Aidan's name—that name was familiar to Spero. He often saw the boy talking to animals and most insects. He knew Aidan didn't care for spiders but that was understandable. Who ever liked spiders, either in a forest setting or crawling on walls in a home?

"I've been thinking about your problem," Spero said.

"What problem?"

"You know … catching the honey cells thrown from the hive. I have a solution."

"Tell me please. It's important," Greeney said.

"If I start right now, I can weave a web to act as a safety net near the ground. It can catch the honey cylinders."

"No kidding," Greeney said. "But that's a long ways down, don't you think?"

"I'm sure it will work. But the drones doing the work must aim precisely for the center of the web."

Spero assured Greeney he'd reinforce the center of the web, doubling the silk threads to hold like iron pins. His silk thread was known as the strongest fiber found anywhere. It carried a lifetime warranty.

"Wonderful, Spero; that's your good deed for the night."

Spero saw it first. He raised one leg to point out the milk weed patch. Two caterpillars gorged themselves on the leaves. They gobbled up the stuff. Spero tasted it himself in a weak moment. It tasted worse than wild artichoke. Greeney agreed the leaves had a toxic taste but that's what helped caterpillars ward off unfriendly stalkers. The leaves gave bad breath.

Spero encouraged Greeney to go join her friends. He promised to finish the safety web before morning—Spider's honor.

As Greeney approached the patch of milkweed, she called out. She didn't want to scare the others when she lumbered close to them in the dark.

"Hi, cousins, I'm delighted to see two of my kind."

They stopped chewing, pleased to see a friendly face. "Hello, cousin," one of them answered, "Who are you?"

Greeney told them her name. She explained how taking time off from work was difficult. As a baker bee's assistant in the hive up the tree, she said she didn't have much time to spare. In fact she was playing hooky this minute.

The two caterpillars were intrigued to meet someone who worked in a bakery. Their life on the ground was rather dull. They wished they had anything to do besides eating. So Greeney offered them a job to replace her when she quit Kendal's bakery. Her friend, the baker bee, needed help, mixing batter and transporting baked goods throughout the hive. If they were interested—

"Tell us when we start. We'll be there," they answered.

"I'll give you adequate notice when it's time to report for work. Got it?" Greeney asked.

"You have a deal."

For four hours Greeney consumed milkweed leaves. She left her cousins in order to arrive in the hive before the twenty-five drones went into action. On her return, she passed by the spot where Spero was spinning; he was involved with gymnastic routines weaving silk threads into a safety net. Greeney complimented Spero. He was a master, threading an intricately designed web. She wondered if she'd be as agile when the time came for her to weave her cocoon.

Returning to Zoey's hive, Greeney heard the snorers storing up energy for another day. The morning promised to be a lively time.

# Chapter Twelve

# Slippery Honey Slide

The morning light introduced a new day. Splotches of muted colors, reds, greens and oranges, painted the sky in the east. Aidan's soft mattress was no comfort to Heydog. He twisted and turned all night. He was the only one in the Bright household who knew a honey collection picnic was in the making. Finally, Heydog grew impatient; he must tell someone or he might wet the bed. Off he jumped, landing with a thump. He patted into the kitchen.

"I thought so," he murmured as he heard the kick steps of the canary who was hopping about on gravel at the bottom of his cage. "You're awake. I hear you."

"Who wants to know?" the canary called down in the dull light.

"It's me, Heydog."

"Oh great, you're the only one I ever talk to except for the little drone. He stopped by to see Aidan the other day. He's a good guy for an insect."

"You're on target, sweet bird. I want to talk to you about Kendal. You always share your news with me. I have a scoop for you."

Heydog told the canary what he knew about Kendal's efforts to help Aidan's family. As he finished, the kitchen lights snapped on. Mrs. Bright staggered in, half asleep. She couldn't understand why Heydog stood up on his hind legs with his nose pressing against the bars of the bird cage. *Peculiar position but no harm done,* she thought.

Mrs. Bright sent Heydog to fetch Aidan. Maybe, scratching on the bed might convince Aidan to get up. Mrs. Bright was frustrated, battling both kids to get up each morning. A cup of coffee got her moving. Keeping Mrs. Bright company, the canary sang out more beautifully than ever, especially before breakfast. Mrs. Bright doubted Heydog did anything to influence the canary's genial disposition.

Heydog returned to the kitchen alone, a defeated beagle.

"Kim … Aidan," Mrs. Bright called loudly, in a cheerful voice. "Rise and shine. It's time for breakfast."

Aidan resisted the call with groggy grunts and groans. Kim pulled the blanket over her head. She turned over on her stomach when she heard her name called and promptly fell back to sleep. Mrs. Bright tried three more times. No success. Discouraged, she went into each of their rooms and yanked off the covers.

"Oh no, Mom," Aidan yelled with one eye open. "It's not morning, is it?"

"Come on, Aidan, there's work to do."

Kim struggling to wake up begged. "Mom, five more minutes. Please."

Mrs. Bright insisted; breakfast was ready. There were chores to do before going on their picnic. Her 10:00 a.m. appointment with Ron meant they'd better hurry to reach the old oak tree on time. A half hour later, they climbed onto the wagon pulled by their old horse. Fortunately he was wide awake. Aidan drove.

"Get up, Mosey. Let's burn up the road." Off they rolled noisily on rattling wheels.

Aidan's mother sang as her troubles faded in a ray of hope. Today promised to be a special one for the family. She hoped!

\*\*\*

Two miles away, Zoey's worker bees were already scattered, searching distant fields for pollen.

Greeney found Kendal alone in the bakery, stacking bread pans on the shelves.

"Good morning, Kendal," Greeney said as she reported her news. "I found my replacement, two caterpillars. They're ready to go to work."

"Wonderful, Greeney," Kendal replied. "It will take two to do as much work as you do."

"Thanks for saying that, Kendal. I met Spero last night. He volunteered to help. He worked all night to construct a safety web, strong enough to catch the honey cylinders."

Kendal sighed with relief. Greeney solved a difficult problem. Now they were ready to drop the cylinders—the last piece of the puzzle.

Twenty-five drones clustered near the hive entrance. They were waiting for orders. Three drones with 20/20 eye sight were assigned as droppers. The other drones flexed their new found muscles and carted cylinders to a point directly above the web. They arranged the cylinders along a single line.

Kendal gave the order, "Let's go, team. Push when ready."

Aiming carefully, the droppers kicked the cylinders off the limb, one after the other. They missed once. A dropper grabbed at his head as he kicked a cylinder. After that one miss, the routine worked splendidly with all honey cylinders landing in the center of the web.

From the tree limb, Kendal peered down. He noticed Spero spreading blades of grass aside. He was monitoring the drones' progress. Leave it to a skillful spider to inspect his handiwork. Satisfied, Spero disappeared.

"That's the last one," a drone yelled.

"Dead eye," roared another. "Hey, guys, we almost batted a thousand."

Handy spoke up. He invited his brothers to meet him in the bakery for a pastry party ... muffins, cakes and bread ... all made with new recipes too.

A rattling noise caught their attention. Kendal knew the sound. It was Aidan's old wagon with a loose wheel. Out of the trees, the Brights came into view.

"Great timing," Kendal declared. "Let's wait here and watch the action."

Heydog alertly stood on his hind legs in back of the wagon. He saw a mound of honey. Roaring out his 'ArRoooo,' he barked. He leaped from the wagon charging at the honey pile.

"My goodness!" Mrs. Bright exclaimed as Aidan applied the brakes and ordered Mosey to stop.

"What's Heydog's problem?" Aidan asked.

Mrs. Bright, Aidan and Kim climbed down to inspect Heydog's discovery. A large pile of honey cylinders caught in a huge spider web. Only one cylinder stood by itself, three feet from the web.

Mrs. Bright shook her head in disbelief; she was stunned. There had to be an explanation.

"Mom, this is the tree where my drone friend lives." Aidan yelled as he pointed. "Look up there." Mrs. Bright and Kim stared in disbelief. A gang of drones waved to them with their wings flapping wildly. Kendal waved so hard he lifted off the ground. He descended to greet Aidan, his mother and his sister. Landing on Heydog's head, Kendal whispered in his ear. "Good dog, there's more to come." Pecking each person on the nose, Kendal returned to the limb, going inside the hive with the drones following.

"Thanks," Aidan hollered. "I know who planned this surprise."

What a shock to find free honey. Mrs. Bright believed she owed someone gratitude for stockpiling a supply of honey under the tree. She urged Aidan and Kim to gather the cylinders and stack them neatly in the back of the wagon. She was glad she hadn't unloaded the plastic bags she bought at the store. They came in handy.

Mrs. Bright glanced at her watch … only five minutes to meet Ron at the old oak tree. As they rode off, Heydog snuggled his head on Mrs. Bright's lap. His sharp eyesight made this pick up possible.

Only a dozen puddle jumps away, Mame and Dame ran around the hive basement making last minute preparations. They were in charge of the tag teams to move 470 pounds of honey.

All twenty UBS teams were accounted for. Mame reminded them that many of their queen sisters stayed up all night to help. They worked in shifts to sharpen the edges of the honey cylinders so they would slide easily down the chute. If a cylinder tipped over, not to worry. Each was sturdy enough to tumble to a safe landing.

Dame issued final instructions. In her role as official referee, Dame assigned work to the tag teams. After selecting a cylinder, they were told to use whatever method worked best for them … push or pull … kick or roll … to move the cylinder onto the chute. On her count 1 2 3—on 3, let it go. The cylinder would slide down the shoot. "Got the procedure right, ladies?" Mame asked.

"We've got it," one vivacious queen responded. "Give us the word, Dame. We'll launch one after the other. The United Bee Service will deliver on time. C'mon, ladies. Sing it out … *UBS, UBS, do or BUST.*"

Mame positioned herself at a tiny window in the bark above the storage area. The view from there was perfect to observe how well the collection effort progressed. She called to Dame. "Fire twenty cylinders. Twenty's plenty to send a message."

Dame gave the tag teams the order. "Fire one … now. Then hold your fire, ladies." The system worked splendidly.

Ron reclined on the grass, waiting for Mrs. Bright. … Pop … pop … pop. … He thought hunters were stalking prey near by.

Instead, honey cylinders dropped out of the base of the old oak tree. A strange sight. He called to Mrs. Bright coming along with the children. He urged her to hurry. Aidan jumped down and ran over to count the containers, exactly twenty.

"Someone's playing a joke on us—the kind I like!" exclaimed Mrs. Bright.

Mame called to Dame to release five more cylinders. Out they shot.

"Kim, you and Aidan better get the plastic grocery bags out of the wagon. I don't know what's coming next."

Mrs. Bright's eyes beamed. Was this for real? She watched as a steady stream of cylinders dropped on the grass. There were so many, that everyone pitched in to catch them in grocery bags and load the bags on the wagon.

One member of a tag team missed her cue. She pulled when pushed worked better. "Oh no," she yelled as she was mowed down, dragged unmercifully downward as the cylinder picked up momentum. By her slick maneuvering, the queen rearranged her body to sit on top of the cylinder. She rode it, as if she was coasting on a sled. At the bottom, she fell into a plastic bag.

Aidan's quick eyes saw the queen tumble into the bag he held tightly. He rushed to retrieve the queen, picked her up, checked for mobility and released her into the air. As the error prone queen arrived back on the limb, her sisters teased her for misfiring.

The Bright family hustled to keep up with the many cylinders popping out of the trunk of the old oak tree. Once Heydog learned the routine, he waited for a plastic bag to fill up; he picked it up and carried the bag to drop it behind the wagon. Ron lifted the bags and packed them neatly on the wagon. Mrs. Bright was astounded to see so many bags of honey.

High in the tree, the UBS queens did all the grunt work, pushing and pulling, kicking and rolling honey cylinders. The tag teams competed with each other to see which team dispensed the most.

Finally, Aidan's mom took a breather as the barrage of cylinders ceased. She looked up. Dozens of queen bees wearing long silky white beards peered down—most were well-groomed except for a few, still wet with suds from their shampoos at the beauty shop.

No one was happier than Aidan's mom. She waved to the bees triumphantly. She held her two fingers in the form of a V, thanking the queen bees. Nodding, the queens paraded inside.

Kendal arrived as Aidan's family climbed into the wagon. He buzzed down, landing on Aidan's shoulder. To prove his friendship, he nestled for a moment in the crook of Aidan's neck. He then skipped over to Heydog, to give him a message. "You did your job, old buddy. Keep your eyes open on the way home. Good dog."

Mrs. Bright thanked Ron for meeting them. With this honey ready for market, the family had no reason to sell the property. As Kendal listened, he heard Mrs. Bright tell Ron that the scientist from the University called her. The preliminary analysis indicated the ingredients of the tiny cake sample produced a health food for bees to ward off disease and mites. The scientist advised Mrs. Bright that she struck gold. The distribution possibilities were unlimited. Bee keepers wherever they tended honey bees needed the new product. This was the news Kendal hoped for … a long term solution to Mrs. Bright's financial problems.

Before Ron departed, Mrs. Bright complained about the lack of rain and the terrible heat. 105 temperatures were forecasted, a furnace for whoever lived in this part of Virginia.

As Aidan's family returned home with a wagon half full of honey, they sang … "It's a grand day for singing, the sky is flying high" … those were the last words Kendal heard. Voices were lost in the trees.

"Kendal," Queen Victoria called from her perch on the limb. "Come join us."

Up he flew, satisfied with the events of the day. The queens admitted that giving was better than receiving.

Queen Victoria, hoping for a compliment, asked Kendal,

"How did we do, Kendal?"

"Queen Victoria, you and the queens showered your royal favors on others today. You have to be proud of yourselves. Your generosity is appreciated. I thank you on behalf of the Brights who love bees."

"You're welcome. By the way, Kendal, reserve the day after tomorrow for an amateur performance. We're planning a fashion show. That's a compromise instead of setting up a charm school near the beauty shop. If you remember, the queens were debating the issue the day you appeared before the Council to make a case for the honey contribution."

"Why do retirees need a fashion show, Grandmother?" Kendal asked Leah.

"The queens love to dress up," Leah said, "in their finest outfits. They love to promenade around the hall."

Although he made a mental note to remember the date, Kendal was preoccupied. He was worried about Tee. He needed to check for any news about the spy mission. As Kendal took his leave, each of the queens hugged him. 303 hugs were too many even for a healthy drone.

Waiting anxiously outside Zoey's hive, a contingent of drones met Kendall at the entrance. They were whooping it up—slap happy jostling, silly as can be. They were determined to identify which one of them missed the target during the dropping exercise. Handy admitted he made the mistake; he was only trying to hold his toupee in place.

That evening as the sky fuzzed and turned dark, a vicious heat wave moved in. Sleep came naturally as bees in both hives finally relaxed after a trying day.

***

The ride home from the old oak tree turned into a bonanza for Aidan's family. Tottering along at a slow pace with a collection of 500 pounds of honey, Aidan's mom exclaimed. "Look! What's that? Did someone leave recyclable plastics and trash to be picked up?"

Aidan slowed the wagon to climb down. "It's a pile of honey combs, Mom; kind of dumb to dump them here."

Further on, there were two separate piles of honeycomb. Aidan braked the wagon once more. He handed the honeycomb to his mother. As they moved along, every hundred feet, more piles of honeycomb laced the ground.

"Mom," Aidan said, "This honey was left here on purpose. Did local bees know we needed help?"

"Yes, Aidan. I suspect they did. Why don't you and Heydog scout along the pathway. Make sure we don't miss any? Honey's too valuable to waste."

"Great idea, Mom. C'mon, Heydog." Aidan searched the area and found more deposits, each one piled neatly. By the time they arrived home, the Brights were exhausted; Heydog panted, and Mosey whinnied under the weight. Aidan's mom estimated they had doubled the pounds of honey she needed to pay the bills for a month.

Following a path cutting through their own 140 hives, they came upon very small mounds of honey cylinders. Handfuls lay on the ground, next to each hive—her own bees appreciated the family too. Every colony scraped up a bit of extra honey to participate in the collection effort.

Mrs. Bright calculated that her own bees collected an extra hundred pounds of honey. As tired as they were, they worked together to load the wagon for the third time. Mrs. Bright backed the wagon into the garage. No unloading till tomorrow. The family needed a breather.

What a rewarding day for the Brights. Elsewhere, dark clouds were gathering.

# Chapter Thirteen

# Killer Bees Plot Plans

Timidly, one of Yoodle's bodyguards knocked on her door, "Your Highness, a scout reported seeing a strange sight up north."

"All right, stupid, tell me."

"I can read it to you, Your Highness." She feared for her life if she made a mistake. "Oh tripe's!" Yoodle blared out, "Come inside and read it."

The guard dragged her feet, taking two steps inside the room.

"Your Highness, the report reads: *This morning all hives up north dumped honey cylinders outside their hives. Piles littered the ground. Shortly, three people in a wagon drove by. They stopped to pick up the honey. They carted it away.*"

Yoodle's anger surged to a breaking point. "Dang those darn bees!" she exclaimed. "Imagine, giving away honey when our food stores are empty." Her stores clerk reported shortages of everything. She must soon find more provisions. She couldn't delay wrapping up the plan to destroy Zoey's colony.

As Yoodle headed for the door, she gaped at the most beautiful queen she ever saw. "Oh no, I see a spot." No flaw was acceptable. She polished her mirror. Satisfied, she moved into the hallway. As Yoodle paced back and forth, a drone stumbled in her way. She aimed and kicked, landing her foot squarely on the drone's snoot. He was bowled over. As he squirmed out of reach, he picked himself off the floor without complaint.

All the lieutenants waited nervously in their assigned seats as prescribed by Yoodle's Rules book. War planning meetings left lieutenants more riled up than war itself. One of the bees at the door called, "Attention," as the Queen stomped into the hall carrying a clip board. She had assignments for the lieutenants. They sprang to their feet, standing rigidly still until the queen mounted the raised platform. "At ease," she howled; they collapsed on their rears.

Queen Yoodle snapped at a guard. "Get Tee," she ordered. "Bring him here."

Tee was dragged to a designated spot in the center of the room to await interrogation. With confidence, he waited. Tee understood how this queen's mind worked. She expected Tee to shake all over as her subjects did in her presence.

"Tee, tell us all you know. I want an accurate picture of Zoey's hive. Don't hold back." Yoodle gave Tee an ultimatum. Nothing less than one hundred percent cooperation was expected.

Tee's eyes surveyed the room. Each of the lieutenants fixed her eyes on him. Tee braced his shoulders and raised his head as high as possible. He made up his mind not to appear intimidated; he stared right back at the lieutenants.

"What can I tell you, Your Highness?" Tee asked, emphatically pronouncing the 't' in highnest. Tee obliged Yoodle … if she wanted a 't' in her title; she got it, and a special brand of Tee to contend with too.

"For starters," she roared, "where's Zoey's hive located … how large is it … what schedule do the bees follow … are they expecting an attack?"

Tee was satisfied. The questions were all answerable. As Yoodle berated Tee, he spotted Louisi, his dungeon companion, in the front row. She smiled as he recited only the facts:

"Zoey's hive isn't far south of the old oak tree … a population of 40,000 bees … most worker bees leave for the fields early in the morning after a daily briefing by their Queen … they leave for work, leery that killer bees are sneaking around in the territory."

Yoodle favored short answers and Tee breezed through her questions without unnecessary detail. For now she was satisfied to let him live long enough to bake cakes and muffins. Her chef was missing after failing at every try to please her.

"All right, Tee, tell me more about Zoey."

The time was right for Tee to start his theatrics. First, he gave Yoodle wild compliments to soften her up. Mixed in with the compliments were insults. Not too many; there was danger in being too critical.

"Queen Zoey is a popular ruler," Tee said. "She's getting older. But her kindness and behavior endear her to all the worker bees, even to the drones."

"You're crazy. You have that wrong, Tee," Yoodle said. "Drones don't have any feelings, except for new queens."

"I'm sorry, Your Highest," Tee apologized, faking remorse, "but drones do care for Queen Zoey."

"Go on. Go on. Time's wasting. Tell me about the conditions in Zoey's hive," she demanded, not believing any queen bee ruled with kindness.

Tee told her how Queen Zoey modernized an inactive bakery and sent a young drone, named Kendal, to school to become a baker bee, so other drones might be trained later. Kendal and Zoey earned a reputation as the drones' champions. In fact, Queen Zoey earned the respect of the entire colony.

"You're overdoing it, Tee," Yoodle interrupted. "Pure nonsense. No queen bee can expect respect from her subjects. Queens can't be involved in a popularity contest."

"Your Highnest," Tee continued, realizing the floor under his feet was getting too slippery. "Bees love Zoey; she encourages kindness in her hive." Tee stole a quick glance at Louisi who winked at him. She got the message. Tee was sure he had one ally in the room.

Tee ducked just in time. Yoodle threw her clip board at him. It narrowly missed his head. Wasting her time was not acceptable. She turned her attention to her war plan. Her army was prepared to attack in three days using their usual tactics. Zoey's hive was their prime target; stealing the honey inventory was next in line of priority.

"That's one consolation," one lieutenant mumbled.

"Quiet in the ranks," Yoodle commanded. One of Louisi's two collaborators whispered to no one in particular, "Yak, Yak, she sure knows how to yak."

"Shhh, shhh," no one in particular silenced her.

Yoodle explained their strategy—swoop down and crash through the hive entrance. Any bees resisting were to be killed. She didn't trust her lieutenants. They were ordered to remain near her as observers, prepared to take charge only if she let them out of her sight.

Louisi raised her hand to be recognized. "Your Highnest, I have a question."

"I see you learned your manners after spending the night with Tee in the dungeons. All right, ask your question. Be quick," Queen Yoodle said. She made a mental note to punish lieutenants more often. An overnight stay in the dungeon made lieutenants more willing to obey, blindly. Louisi's humility proved to Yoodle the value of punishment.

"What do we do with the prisoners?" Louisi asked.

The answer was clear. Queen Zoey and Kendal were to be placed in solitary confinement. The drones were to be executed. Worker bees were to be assigned to menial work, to clean the latrines and to cart off dead bodies.

Yoodle checked to see if Tee dared stay in the room after she tossed the clipboard at him. He hadn't budged. "Now, Tee, tell me more about the bakery in the hive."

What a great excuse for Tee to boast how Kendal became the drones' inspiration. Kendal helped anyone in need. At this moment, Kendal was assisting a family of beekeepers up north with financial problems.

"Those hives up north," Yoodle prompted. "Do they belong to the boy who roams around the forest talking to animals?"

"Yes, Your Highnest, the same boy. His name is Aidan. He rescued Kendal and now they are best friends."

"I want to meet this Kendal," Yoodle said, "before I sting him and put him to sleep forever. Maybe I'll save a stinger dose for the kid too." She dismissed the lieutenants, ordering Tee to wait.

"Tee, bake me more cakes and muffins. Get busy, hmm ... baker bee you be ... I'll expect them delivered by noon. Don't be late. Got it?"

"I do, Your Highnest."

"Now, get out of my sight."

Tee hid from Yoodle, his mission accomplished. At the right time, he planned to escape. To return home with Yoodle's war plans to attack Zoey's hive completed his assignment. Before he made his break though, Tee resolved to concoct a recipe Yoodle would remember as long as she lived.

# Chapter Fourteen

# Hot Time Is Brewing

Out of her deep sleep, Zoey jumped up, jolted awake by her jumping legs. She dreamt she was kicking honey cylinders helping the drones. She arose to go check outdoors. A few clouds drifted from east to west, blotting out the bright moon. Zoey's forecast yesterday was on target. No rain again today; temperature rising to a boiling 105 degrees. Her prediction technique was more accurate than radio reports.

A pulsating light drew Zoey's attention. She knew hunters loitered there, camping in the trees. *If they'd only go home,* she thought. Looking north, she admired the outline of the barren old oak tree. Its tired limbs reached longingly for the sky above.

So many things to be thankful for ... her son already won the heart of the retirees; he earned the respect of drones and Aidan's family. Kendal's greatest challenge ahead was to gain confidence of worker bees. They only knew him by reputation as a baker bee who made delicious baked goods. They hadn't yet experienced his kindness because they were bustling about, busy at their many tasks. Zoey pondered on her coming retirement. Maybe tomorrow she'd make the announcement.

As she paced the floor, Zoey stewed. The killer bees' invasion was coming soon. Hopefully, Tee's report would provide accurate intelligence about their plans. She must prepare her colony to swarm and seek safety elsewhere. Through Kendal's contact with the Brights, she knew there were empty hives near Aidan's house. Zoey was certain the Brights had room for her family.

"Queen Zoey, are you up?" Rebecca called from the hallway. "Kendal is here with breakfast."

"Oh yes, Rebecca. I'm hungry as usual. Ask him to come in."

"Greeney is with him. Can she join you?"

"Of course, all three of you. Let's have breakfast together."

Queen Zoey invited them to sit down. She served.

"My goodness," said Greeney, "this is the first and last time a queen will be my servant."

"Why do you say that?" Zoey asked.

"Today I leave to spin my cocoon. It's the final stage before I become a butterfly; it's the reason I came into this world. Before I leave, Queen Zoey, I'm pleased to report I located replacements to help Kendal in the bakery. I'll get word to them to report for work before I leave."

"We're going to miss you, Greeney," Zoey acknowledged. "We enjoy your lively nature, your excellent work and those fancy dancing routines. I'm sure your future will be a bright one."

"Now, Rebecca, what are you doing today?" Zoey asked as she split a muffin in two to determine its flavor. Ah! Lemon, a wee bit tart, but tasty.

Rebecca answered with mischief in her eyes. "Something tells me I'll be escorting my favorite queen to lay eggs."—Rebecca laughed. "Whatever you want me to do, my queen, I'm at your service."

"How well I know, Rebecca. No queen has a more faithful companion." Zoey instructed Rebecca to be ready to lead the colony in a grand swarm to occupy a new hive. She also advised Rebecca about vacant hives near Aidan's home. They both knew worker bees raved about the flowery fields there. Kendal and Rebecca noticed that Zoey ran out of breath, grappling for the right words.

"Something is bothering you, Mother," Kendal said. "I can tell. You're preoccupied this morning."

"You're right, Kendal. This is my last day to lay eggs for the colony. I'm frazzled, totally worn out. I must tell the truth."

*** 

Miles away in Yoodle's hive, thousands of killer bees were fired up. Their anger erupted as they squabbled with each other. They were driven into a growing frenzy by nasty lieutenants. For no acceptable reason, the lieutenants issued contradictory orders, making worker bees run into each other. That's what Yoodle delighted to see … confusion and conflict.

At Yoodle's direction, Tee remained at his post all night, locked in Yoodle's private kitchen. Intent on gaining her favor, Tee prepared the tastiest honey muffin mix imaginable. However, he added one twist not listed in the recipe; he salted the batter with droppings swept up from the floor, even dust from behind the oven. Tee thought his batter was a fitting tribute to satisfy her taste buds. He disguised the gobs of waste and junk he collected. Ugh! What a messy mess. He must be careful not to let Yoodle suspect anything. She might make him taste the muffins before she ate one.

One of Yoodle's bodyguards barged into the kitchen. She grabbed Tee by the scuff of his neck. "Get a move on; you're summoned to serve the Queen."

Tee picked up the tray of muffins and cakes, and obeyed. As he followed the bodyguards, he checked on the layout of the hive. When the time came for his escape, he must speed through the hallways and out the exits. A clear path might give him a head start.

At the podium, Yoodle presided over the war planning meeting of her lieutenants. Without apology, she did all the talking. All eyes fixed on her face. Anyone losing eye contact might be in for a tongue lashing or a punishment far worse.

"Here's what we'll do," Yoodle dictated. She spelled out her plan, drawing a diagram pinpointing a large elm tree within one mile of Zoey's hive. Using the elm tree as base of operations ... Yoodle sensed a distraction as she issued her orders.

"Tee, pay attention. I see you at the door with my breakfast. Bring it here. Be quick, Tee. Answer me, is there a hallway inside the hive entrance?" she demanded.

"No, Your Highnest," Tee replied, pretending to be afraid. Edging closer, he needed to learn every bit of the war plan. He described the inside of the hive in minute detail. The main hall consisted of one large open room with vertical honey combs. Upstairs housed the royal bedroom and space for the attendants. In the basement the bakery sign was prominently displayed. It read 'Kendal's Kitchen,' and next door was the cafeteria.

"Is that what you wanted to know, Your Highnest?"

Without acknowledging Tee's description, Yoodle continued. "Don't you see, lieutenants, how easy it is to obtain information from a captive who's shaking in his boots?"

Tee grasped the tray tightly so as not to—carefully he placed the baked goods in front of Yoodle. To dump the goodies in her lap was awfully tempting. "There's a secondary target, Your Highnest." Tee mumbled so low only Yoodle heard the comment.

"What? What did you say?" Yoodle screamed. "Where? What else is there? Spit it out, Tee."

Tee purposefully gave his academy award winning performance. He shook all over; his legs quivered and his wings fluttered, to prove how fearful he was. "Queen Yoodle, if you go directly north from Zoey's hive, there's a dead old oak tree where hundreds of bees live. They have a large supply of honey in their inventory."

"Good!" Yoodle exclaimed, as she spit out a messy glob of

muffin with floor droppings visible in the mess. "We'll kill two hives with one swarm. We want to go north anyway, to conquer the hives surrounding Aidan's house."

"Lieutenants … the old oak tree will be the next target. We'll use the same strategy … worker bees first with drones carrying supplies … lieutenants to follow … and I'll follow with my two bodyguards." Then for no good reason, Yoodle threw the tray on the floor.

As Tee retrieved the tray, he breathed easily. He had the whole attack plan, the solid intelligence he came to gather.

"Tee, get out of my sight. Go." Yoodle ordered. "Make me two dozen muffins for later. I don't know what you added in your muffin batter. But it tasted terrific. Make sure you double the next batch. Get moving."

Tee skipped along on his merry way to continue his work in the bakery. He predicted confusion the next morning when Yoodle issued orders to attack. That was a great opportunity to make his escape. But first he must fix Yoodle before going to bed. He must bake a special batch of pastries. Using a mix of the foulest ingredients, Tee planned to throw her digestive system out of kilter. When she vomited, the smell would give her pause to remember Tee, her temporary baker bee.

# Chapter Fifteen

# Calamity in the Making

While their Queen ate breakfast, the worker bees waited for the morning briefing. They babbled on about dandelion punch, clover odor, or this or that—regular grapevine gossip. One worker summed up their spirit. "Ladies," she exhorted them, "let's swing and do our thing." They chuckled as Queen Zoey promenaded into the hall.

Zoey noticed that all the worker bees were in exceptional spirits, anxious to go to work. This attitude wasn't common in other hives she knew about. Zoey scanned the assembly. They were all her children. Silently, she whispered her blessings on them.

"My dears," she called for their attention. "I congratulate you. Because of your hard work, yesterday we shared part of our extra honey with a deserving family. They are bee keepers who show an abiding love for bees. I know they provide the most modern and clean hives for their colonies. The colonies are protected from disease and from raiders who come to steal their honey."

Kendal smiled when he heard Zoey's words. What a clever

way to prepare the workers as they swarmed. With information about vacant hives near Aidan's house, they might be inclined to swarm to one of them.

Zoey had checked on today's weather. Her forecast was hot as a furnace, no rain in sight. If the air seemed calm, the wind still threatened to whip up any time. She suggested all workers quit early and return home to cool off.

Greeney circulated around the hall carrying extra provisions for the worker bees. Kendal anticipated them to show up to eat before going to the fields. Everyone dashed for the pastries.

With moistened eyes, the Queen asked for silence. "My dear family tomorrow is an important day. I'll make important announcements. Please come early for my briefing. Now have a nice day."

✳✳✳

Two hours later, the deer hunters packed up their tent and rifles. When they awoke this morning, they were drenched in sweat. Time to go home. Carefully, they doused the cooking fire with water. One thoughtfully threw dirt on the embers. As they left for home, one hunter carelessly tossed his cigarette on the ground, stomping on the butt, but without grinding it into the dirt. Within minutes, a trailing cigarette smoke curled upward, the butt still alive and dangerous.

Ashes smoldered, gasping for new life. A fire kicked into motion. It spread westward, driven by a sudden wind burst through the dried hay. Soon a thick cloud of smoke penetrated the hive. The fire burned itself out quickly as it collided with a hill of clay. With the fire out, the smoke had done its job. It circulated through the main floor.

No smoke reached 'Kendal's Kitchen.' Both bakers, Kendal and Greeney, were scurrying around their shop, creating a new line of cakes and muffins using Martha's recipes. As Bookie read one recipe out loud, Handy experimented with proportions of nectar and pollen powder, mixed with pure honey. The drones made dozens and dozens of loaves of honey bread, brown and crusty.

Kendal checked the time. "Ready, Greeney? The Queen has been laying eggs long enough. Let's bring her a treat. How's a crunchy honey crumb cake sound to you? C'mon, Greeney, shake a leg … a few of your legs at least."

Greeney grunted under the strain of a tight saddle bag. She followed Kendal upstairs. They both gagged as they detected a terrible odor. Kendal scampered forward to find Queen Zoey prone on the floor, with Rebecca and other attendants knocked out around her. No one moved. No visible sign of life.

"Greeney, are they dead? My, oh my. I must find help. Zoey and the others need medical attention. I know. I'll find Aidan. He works around hives and has seen his bees knocked out. Stay here, Greeney. Guard the hive. I'll hurry."

Without waiting for a reply, Kendal bolted for the entrance. Racing through the air, he hardly noticed the old oak tree as he flashed by it. Hay fields near by were singed, burnt black. He flew higher, to escape the odor.

Over the next two miles, he traveled north at breathtaking speed. Kendal hoped for the best. Queen Zoey and the others must be revived. Nearing Aidan's house, bees in a number of hives below spotted him and took chase. He zigzagged, flying around and through bushes to evade his pursuers. Finally, he sailed beneath the wagon and lost the others. His wings gave out; Kendal fell flat on his face in the grass in Aidan's yard.

Luckily, Heydog watched the chase from the porch. He hooted and cheered Kendal on as he evaded enraged bees on his tail. He ran over and slumped on his stomach with his nose smelling Kendal for life. He urged the drone to grab an ear. With Kendal hanging on, Heydog carried him to Aidan's front door. Although weak, Kendal explained his situation.

After hearing the story, Heydog scratched madly on the screen to get Aidan's attention. Aidan turned and saw the little drone hanging on by a hair; he dropped his peanut butter and jelly sandwich as he rushed for the door.

"Oh, no!" he exclaimed. Aidan gently nudged Kendal to climb onto his finger. He brought the exhausted drone to the kitchen table. "What's wrong?" Aidan asked.

*What's wrong?* Kendal let the question repeat in his head as his fears ripped him apart. He sighed so deeply, it made his side hurt. He understood what was wrong. His problem was asking for help. Heydog knew the whole story, but he didn't know how to tell Aidan either.

Aidan's mother arrived home from the fields. She saw Aidan staring at the drone on the kitchen table. "What happened to your little friend?" she asked.

"I don't know, Mom. He hasn't moved. At this rate, he'll sleep forever."

"Let me look, Aidan." As Mrs. Bright examined the drone, she caught a whiff of smoke. She understood. She ran to fetch a dish; she mixed a few granules of sugar with drops of water. With an eye dropper his mother gave him, Aidan encouraged Kendal to take a taste. Slowly, Kendal wiggled his head; he heard Mrs. Bright repeat how she used sugar and water to wake Kendal.

The answer to his problem clicked. Spreading his wings full out, he fluttered them in gratitude. He pecked Aidan on the nose, not forgetting his mother. As Aidan opened the door, Kendal soared away. He flew even faster on the return flight.

Aidan threw his arms around his beagle's neck. "Heydog," Aidan said. "You're the greatest. Thanks for rescuing the drone. He seems O.K. Let's follow him, to make sure."

The two mile course was familiar to Aidan and Heydog. They knew all the shortcuts.

Greeney was pacing as Kendal landed. "Come on, Greeney. I know what to do." Together, they dashed for the bakery. There, Kendal mixed honey and water, rushed upstairs with the liquid sloshing out of the saddlebag pockets. They lifted Zoey, propped her up and dribbled liquid into her mouth. They used the same procedure for each of the other sleeping beauties. Queen Zoey stirred first. She struggled to stand up, groggy from the dense smoke. Hacking, the others staggered to their feet.

"Kendal, you saved us," Zoey exclaimed as she planted a big kiss on the top of his head.

Within a half hour, Aidan and Heydog arrived at the old oak tree. Aidan grabbed a low branch and climbed. Reaching the hive entrance, he called inside. "Hello in there. Are you there, little drone?"

Zoey and Kendal shuffled out the entrance with Greeney at their heels. Everything seemed in order to Aidan. Zoey curtsied politely in greeting. Aidan didn't understand her gesture. He never saw a queen curtsy before.

If only Zoey knew how to speak to humans; the little boy deserved her gratitude. He needed to be told how her colony planned to relocate soon, perhaps even to occupy the hive outside Aidan's bedroom. Aidan needed the information to warn his mother to safeguard her hives from rampaging killer bees. Unfortunately, Zoey had no way to speak to people.

But all was well. So Aidan climbed down. He coaxed Heydog to follow him with a promise of some fun. A few frogs lived nearby in a barren brook. They were chronic complainers, croaking about this or croaking about that. They had one legitimate complaint; the shortage of rain made their lives miserable.

Early in the afternoon the worker bees returned from the fields to beat the oppressive heat. A heavy smell of smoke lingered in the hive. "What happened?" they asked each other.

Zoey called everyone to meet her in the briefing hall to explain … how smoke almost killed her and others in the hive … how Kendal saved them all. The worker bees inquired about Kendal's whereabouts. The answer amazed them. Once Zoey was revived, he returned to work in the bakery.

Ten representatives selected by the worker bees, asked to meet with the Queen. They inquired about her health. They proposed that Kendal deserved formal recognition for his good deeds. The stories of his services to all in need were spreading near and far.

"What a wonderful idea," the Queen said. "Tell me what you think is a fitting reward."

Downstairs Kendal hummed; his family was safe and secure. Kendal stacked the oven with unbaked pastries with the help of Handy, Jockie, Bookie and Mechie. Greeney promised to mix one more vat of batter before she departed to locate a hideaway to spin her cocoon. She jogged double time calling to Kendal. "Hey boss, will you sing a duet with me? It may be our last chance."

"By all means, Greeney. Name your tune."

"The song you wrote, Kendal. 'Greeney and Me.'"

As they finished the last refrain, a worker bee skipped into the kitchen.

"Kendal, Queen Zoey requests your presence and the bakery crew too."

"Thank you," Kendal said. "O.K., guys. We're on our way."

As Kendal and the others made their entrance into the great hall, they were stunned by the sight. Not an empty seat in the place; it was packed. *Strange* ... the colony only met for early morning briefings. Here they were, the entire colony, apparently waiting for the drones to join them.

A deafening noise blasted the quiet; it shook the honey combs balanced on their edges outside. There were accolades, applause, cheering, whistling and buzzing sounding from every section of the hall.

Rebecca pushed forward to escort Kendal to the podium. The Queen's face lit up, a smile, a mile wide. She invited Kendal to step up on the platform to be seen by the audience and for him to see the whole assembly. What an impressive view. Forty thousand sets of eyes locked onto a baker bee.

"Son, you'd better sit down," Queen Zoey said as she slid a stool behind him. "For the first time in the history of the bee world," Zoey declared, "worker bees petitioned a queen bee to

honor a drone. They asked you be granted a title of distinction …"
Zoey stopped in the middle of a sentence; she almost forgot the
designated title.

"Therefore, it's my great honor," she continued, "to proclaim,
here in the presence of the entire colony, that you Kendal … for-
evermore … will bear the title of 'Hero of the Hive.'"

The noise in the hall escalated to such a high pitch that a
number of bees struggled to know what to do first. They had to
choose, either to clap or to fold their forelegs over their antennae
to muffle the noise. Shouts reverberating in the hall caused an
echo chamber. Kendal jumped off the stool. Humbly, he bent
from the waist to take a bow. He was truly touched.

When the clamor simmered down, Queen Zoey introduced
Greeney. She balanced uncomfortably on her sixteen legs; she stood
motionless, unsure what to expect. Queen Zoey made it official.
Greeney was departing this evening to spin her cocoon, the final
stage of her transformation to become a butterfly. She proved her
resourcefulness in improving the quality of bee life in the hive.

"Go with our deepest gratitude," Zoey said as she shook six of
Greeney's legs.

Greeney saluted the Queen and started out of the hall.

"Wait for me, Greeney," Kendal called. "How are you doing,
my friend?"

"I'm a bit wobbly," Greeney admitted. "You deserved your
award, you know. You're my hero too, Kendal."

"Why are you insecure, Greeney?"

"My cousins told me to expect a loss of appetite, to watch my
skin turn yellow," she said. When that happened, it was time to
start spinning her cocoon. "I'm nervous, Kendal. Making your
own cocoon terrifies me."

"You'll do fine, Greeney. Bee larvae take to it naturally when
they spin theirs."

Greeney doubted spinning was that easy. She heard many varia-
tions on the cocoon theme … once you started, you spun end-

lessly for three days ... you tied your own silky thread into knots, making a noose to hang yourself from a limb ... you drew the silk from inside your body as you made thousands of turns in midair to build a cocoon ... a few caterpillars became so confused turning and twisting, they tied themselves in a knot and had to start all over again.

"You're right, Greeney. Spinning a cocoon is trying, but every caterpillar on earth goes through metamorphosis."

Greeney feared to face the world alone. She admitted she was spoiled, living in the hive with so many honey bees.

"You'll have other friends," Kendal commented. "Don't worry."

Greeny revealed a caterpillar's secret, how they chose to travel alone except twice a year. On those two occasions, they migrated first north to south and later, back north again, in the same way as human snowbirds do. "Speaking of traveling, Kendal, before I leave, I'll contact my two cousins to report for work."

"Thank you, Greeney. Have them go to the old oak tree in two days. I'll alert Martha that two caterpillars will be reporting to her. Well, old girl, we had wonderful times, you and I. It passed too fast. What words of wisdom can you leave with me?"

Greeney pondered on Kendal's question. She spoke:

> *Knowing is better than not knowing.*
> *Growing is better than shrinking.*
> *Changing is better than not growing.*
> *Believing is more than seeing.*
> *It's at the heart of being.*

"Greeney, I'll have to think about your words for a long time. They're packed with ideas. Someday, I hope to see you again, my friend."

And Greeney departed without another word.

Kendal watched her leave; he was concerned this was the last time he'd see Greeney the Caterpillar. Such a dear friend.

Kendal yawned. Today's activities sapped his energy. He must conserve his strength. His true tests were yet to come.

# Chapter Sixteen

# Defensive Measures

The dwindling smoke made the colony sleep soundly. Only the flapping of many wings worked in exhausting the smell and gray soot from the hive.

When Queen Zoey opened her eyes, she detected a lemon aroma. It reminded her of her favorite muffins next to blueberry. But breakfast must wait. Other more important matters were pressing.

As she paced her chamber, Zoey rehearsed. There was so much for her to say at today's briefing. This was her last appearance. According to habit, she checked the weather. Zoey scooted out on the ledge; she scanned the sky and smelled the air. The air was clear, a wee bit cooler; unfortunately, no chance of rain today.

With a spring in her steps, Zoey headed downstairs—whoops! A collision. Running up the stairs to awaken her, Rebecca bumped into her, head on.

"Good morning, Queen Zoey," Rebecca said, apologizing for running her down. "I hope I didn't hurt you. You're getting an early start this morning."

"Good morning, Rebecca. No damage done. We have a full agenda today. Are you ready?"

"Yes, as ready as I ever will be under the circumstances."

As Zoey mounted the platform, she inhaled a deep breath. "Good day my family." She slurred; her tongue thickened from nervousness. Her family sensed the anxiety. They knew this briefing was to be earth shaking.

Queen Zoey reported the killer bee attack seemed imminent. But Tee's intelligence was expected to reveal the details. The colony certainly owed him thanks for his bravery.

Hesitantly, the Queen told the colony that after the briefing, they must separate from her, once and for all. Leaving the hive was necessary for their safety.

One of the worker bees shouted out, "What's our role in your plans, my Queen?"

Zoey appreciated the question. "Rebecca will organize a swarm. You'll all fly off to find a new hive out of harm's way. Take young Mia with you. She's only two days old but she's been groomed to be your new queen. I saw a few of you chasing Mia, playfully biting her."

From deep in the audience, a childish voice giggled.

"Mia is so young she needs help flying," Zoey said. "I suggest a crew of strong flyers form tightly around her. Carry her, if it's necessary."

"My Queen," the giggler, called from the audience, "what about you?"

"I see you there, Mia. You know a few of the worker bees. Please stand up so every one of my 40,000 children knows you by sight ... thank you."—

Zoey decided to remain with Kendal to finalize their defenses. As she mentioned Kendal's name, she remembered something ... from the top of her lungs, she thanked the colony for its vote of confidence in her son. They deserved the credit for awarding Kendal the title, 'Hero of the Hive.'"

Zoey reminded the assembly of Kendal's friendship with Aidan proved valuable for the entire colony. The fields near his home were rich in pollen and nectar. She then mentioned a hive vacancy located outside Aidan's bedroom window. It was perfect for anyone seeking a fine home, partly shaded, painted white and facing south.

"Thank you, Queen Zoey," a worker bee spoke up. "Isn't there another announcement you intended to make, my Queen? Rumors are running wildly around the hive."

Complete silence filled the hall. Zoey decided to make it official. She was retiring immediately. A room was reserved for her at the queen's retirement hive; one for Kendal too.

The time had come to close the briefing. "My dear family," she said. "You're all my dear children. I don't think I have to explain how much I care for you. I can't possibly tell you individually. I'd be talking for a couple of weeks. I wish you all fulfillment of your dreams. Leave with my fondest best wishes."

One of the twenty-five drones coughed for attention. He asked how the drones fit into the Queen's plans.

"Excellent question, Handy," Zoey responded. She almost forgot the drones in all the excitement. Instead of answering, she invited the drones to stand up in their places. Clustered in three groups of about eight each, she asked them to delay departing; she needed them for special duties. Afterwards, they were free to follow the swarm. Spontaneously, a few drones hooted out their appreciation; high fives broke out in each of the three clusters.

Rebecca spoke in behalf of all the worker bees. "You guys are the greatest. We'll have the welcome mat sitting outside the front door waiting for you."

Queen Zoey's face relaxed. The drones finally were recognized as valuable citizens of the colony.

"I'm afraid it's time, Rebecca. You're dismissed. Go, do good. … Go, swarm. I'll accompany you in spirit."

Rebecca escorted Mia outside; hand in hand they left the hive.

Zoey and Kendal mounted the stairs to the Queen's chamber and stepped out on the ledge. As they peered down, the mass of bees gathered to swarm. Scouts had been assigned earlier to search for a suitable hive.

"Look!" Zoey exclaimed. "The scouts are doing their waggle dance to instruct the swarm ... as to direction, the distance and the desirability of the hive they located. You can see everyone nodding 'yes,'"

On a signal from Rebecca, they ascended as one body in a swirling dark cloud. The swarm took off and flew north.

"Well, Kendal," Zoey said with satisfaction, "The colony is traveling directly for Aidan's house. The swarm wouldn't move so speedily if they were in doubt of their destination."

"It's quite a sight, Kendal," Zoey said with delight. "There's work for us to do." They hurried downstairs, two steps at a time. Sitting at a table, they explored their options.

A pattering sound, like tap shoes on a hard wood floor, broke the silence. Tee smartly marched across the room; he halted and clicked his heels in front of Queen Zoey.

"Agent Tee reporting Your Highness." Tee wasn't kidding; he stood stiffly at attention, proud to complete his spy assignment. "I'm sorry, Queen Zoey. I almost called you, Your Highest. Queen Yoodle demands that title from her subjects."

"Welcome, Tee," Zoey said. She noticed that her secret agent wheezed as he tried to catch his breath. "I'm so relieved to see you're safe and in good health, Tee. I was getting worried about your safety."

Tee provided background for the intelligence he gathered. Narrowly, he missed being trapped in the killer bees' hive. By chance, he met one decent lieutenant by the name of Louisi. She told him two other lieutenants shared her sentiments. All three wanted to desert. By accident, Tee overheard Yoodle issuing an order for him to be exterminated. That's when he made his break. Ready to make his report, Tee inhaled to begin.

"Tee, take your time. Catch your breath," Zoey said as she stroked Tee's head to help him relax.

Tee sucked in his stomach and took three deep breaths … he counted 1, 2, 3. "Here are the orders Yoodle gave her lieutenants." Tee launched into a full report. Step by step, Tee described what Yoodle intended to do tomorrow. That's when the attack was scheduled.

The order was issued by Yoodle for the army to break into three groups, each one responsible for a different area of Zoey's hive … upstairs or downstairs or on the main floor, where the main hall was located. She ordered the Queen and Kendal to be placed under hive arrest. After the battle ended and declared a victory, Yoodle would make her grand entrance surrounded by attendants. She'd claim Zoey's hive as her property.

"Great job of reporting, Tee. It's precise and clear," Kendal said, as he offered his congratulations.

Completely satisfied with Tee's report, Zoey was still concerned about Yoodle's reaction if she found an empty hive. Kendal anticipated that problem. He coached Tee to offer a secondary target. So Tee mentioned the location of the retirees' hive to Yoodle.

"Does Yoodle know who lives there?" Zoey asked. She hoped detailed information was withheld about the 303 queens' secret life.

"No, my Queen," Tee answered. "She only knows that hundreds live there with a huge supply of honey for a rainy day."

Tee's intelligence assignment worked better than a charm. His acting was worth a prize for a superb performance. The colony now knew the whole truth, how Tee only pretended to be a traitor to win Yoodle's confidence.

Kendal sat back, letting Tee bask in the spotlight. Based on Tee's intelligence report, the defense plan for both hives was in good order.

To prepare the best defense, Kendal needed input from all the drones. He sent Tee to round them up. Twenty-five drone heads were better than one. He found the bakery crew—Handy, Jockie, Bookie and Mechie—lounging outside the embalmer's chambers. For want of something better to do, they were counting dead bodies—not many yet, but the coming battle was sure to produce overcrowding.

"C'mon, guys," Tee said. "We have better things to do. Kendal needs us."

As the meeting started, Kendal recapped the situation. The attack was coming in the morning. Their job was to set a trap. Kendal preferred the enemy bees be entrapped rather than killed.

"Or to put it another way," Tee said. "To contain the enemy rather than annihilate them. Right, Kendal?"

"You've got it, Tee," Kendal said as he punched Tee on his foreleg in fellowship.

"Let's hear your suggestions," Kendal urged the drones to speak.

After getting their input, Kendal reviewed the action plan.

"My friends, all sections of the hive must be coated with sticky resin; that's a basic requirement for the plan to work. Mechie, you go to the upper level and build a trap door to close automatically when the invaders storm upstairs. Jockie, I'll need the doorway opening to the balcony barricaded to prevent escape out of Zoey's chamber. When that's done, work with Bookie to install a spring lock on the door going downstairs to trap the enemy invading the bakery."

"Oh, no!" Handy protested. "They'll wreck our kitchen and cafeteria. The equipment will be ruined."

"Good thinking," Kendal responded. "Handy, you bake a batch of special cakes using sleeping powder. Leave the cakes out in the open. The killer bees won't pass them up, I'm sure."

"I'll fix them. Never fear, Kendal." Handy started digging through his recipe book for a lasting delight.

Kendal directed the drones' attention to the main hall where all the honeycomb towers were located. Nothing can be spared.

Each surface in the main hall needs painting or swabbing with sticky adhesive resin. There was a large supply of sticky stuff stored in a reserve tank. Since resin acted as crazy glue, contact automatically snagged anything caught as fly paper traps a fly permanently. If one bee touched another bee, the resin bound the two together, glued tight.

Kendal asked his friends for their reactions. They agreed. Handy shouted, "Whoopee." The plan was airtight.

"We'd better get started," Kendal said. "Once we're finished, Tee will lead all drones to the new hive. Tee, you go to Aidan's house. I'm sure you'll find Zoey's colony near by. Speaking for Queen Zoey and for myself, you proved yourselves again. I'm pleased female worker bees finally respect you. Thanks from the bottom of my heart."

Handy asked one last question. "Don't we need an exit plan? What do we do about the stuck bees and the sticky hive after the first wave attack?"

"Another logical question, Handy," Kendal replied. "I have a plan to address that question. I want to discuss my idea with Queen Zoey. You may have a role in this plan too. I'll let you know. Let's go."

The drone crew went to work. They tapped the resin tank, filling tiny thimbles to be distributed to key locations around the hive. Mechie assembled two hoses, one stretching as far as the upper floor and the other reaching the basement. Once the hoses were in place, Mechie turned on the valves and pumped the resin to both floors. With buckets, four drones carried resin to the others who painted and mopped the surface with sticky resin. The hours passed quickly; they flung their sticky mops and brushes into the hive. Together they flew high in the sky to join Rebecca and the colony at Aidan's house.

Chapter Seventeen

# Queen For A Day

While the drones coated every surface with resin, Kendal and Zoey hesitated at the hive entrance. Leaving their home was hard. Beneath the limb, a sound caught Kendal's attention.

"Look, Mother," he pointed. "There's Aidan. The poor kid is sound asleep at the base of our tree. That's a strange place for him to be at this hour of the morning."

"You'd better see if he's all right, Kendal," Zoey said. "I'm sure his mother doesn't know he's out of the house this early."

Kendal glided down. As he landed lightly on Heydog's ear, the beagle detected an itch. He started to scratch. Kendal yelled, "'Heydog, control yourself. I'm right here on your ear. ... What's Aidan doing out here? He belongs in bed."

Kendal was worried about Mrs. Bright awakening to find Aidan's bed empty. But Kendal underestimated Aidan. Before leaving the house, he left a note. He printed in big letters ...

*Hi Mom.*
*   I took Heydog with me. We're going to see if my drone*
*needs help. Don't worry.*
*Love, Me ... I mean, Aidan.*

"Don't worry, Kendal," Heydog said. "I saw him leave a note near his mother's coffee cup. He came to help you. Tell me, Kendal, how we can repay you for the wagon load of honey?"

"Oh, if I only knew how to speak to Aidan," Kendal said. "I'd ask him to scout the killer bees. If he stayed at a safe distance, he could alert me when they were on the way. They're expected early in the morning. I don't know what time."

"I'll take the assignment," Heydog said. "I can sneak out early and act as your observer. I'll go a mile south. When I see the killer bees, I'll give you a loud 'ArRoooo.'"

With Heydog's help, Kendal was ready. Zoey then surprised Kendal by landing on Heydog's other ear to say hello and add her thanks. Flying backwards as honey bees do, Zoey and Kendal arose and waved goodbye. In no time, they reached the old oak tree. Mame and Dame saw them coming. The news of Zoey's retirement arrived even before Zoey set foot at the retirement hive. As mother and son docked outside, Mame called out.

"Welcome, Zoey and Kendal." The greeting was echoed by Dame. Both wrestler's crunched Kendal in tight hugs as they kissed Zoey hello. The Council members had been walking around on pins and needles, waiting to see them. Mame led the way as Dame shut the front door and locked it.

As Zoey and Kendal entered the Council room, the retirees stood up as one body. They beat their wings to greet Zoey, the youngest queen in the royal line and Kendal, the royal prince.

Victoria called Zoey to the podium.

"Zoey, we're all excited for you to join us in retirement. Here's your badge, number 304. Your mom owns number 303. She'll escort you to the seat of honor. Do you have any words of wisdom for us?"

"Yes, I believe I do," Zoey answered. For the first time as equals, she acknowledged retirement didn't come easy. Didn't they agree? All the retirees giggled in understanding. Zoey was right. They had no responsibility for the lives of a colony, no laying eggs and loads of time to be free and be.

Zoey updated the Council on the dangers of a killer bee invasion. She beckoned Kendal to join her. He told the Council that Tee secured the necessary intelligence about the enemy's attack plan. The attack was scheduled to arrive the next morning. Queen Zoey ordered Rebecca to lead a swarm of her colony to take them out of harm's way. A modern new hive awaited their arrival near Aidan's home.

"Good work," Leah said. She credited her daughter and grandson for their quick thinking. Leah acknowledged a sharp mind was a family trait.

Victoria leaned over to whisper in Martha's ear. "What did Kendal say?"

"Kendal is briefing the queens on what's going on. Isn't he a superb speaker?" Martha said. "He's living proof that drones are valued citizens. Since his arrival in Zoey's hive, Kendal has turned the bees' world upside down."

"Martha, where do you get all your information?" Victoria asked.

"From the delivery bees, Victoria. When they come in the back entrance, they visit my kitchen. They tell me what's happening in local hives. Their reports only trickled in at first, but now I hear bits and pieces of news ten times a day. Only recently, all of Zoey's worker bees acclaimed him as 'Hero of the Hive."

"I call that real news, Martha. Thank you."

"One other thing," Martha added. "Drones from all over are signing a petition asking Kendal to establish a bakers' training school and—"

"Please, Martha, listen. I can't hear him."

Kendal used a corked bottle cap next to the podium as a makeshift peg board. With rose thorns as pins, Kendal marked the position of the enemy and the locations of the two hives. He traced the line of the expected attack using a dried out thorn as a pointer. He told the queens that the initial attack involved an overwhelming force.

To defend against the enemy's movements, the drones pasted the floors, walls and ceilings with resin that sticks better than crazy glue. Kendal predicted all killer bee workers would be stopped on their initial contact. Spontaneously, Kendal and Zoey cracked smiles. They imagined Yoodle's surprise when she found the targeted hive empty.

"Ingenious!" Victoria exclaimed. "What about the rest of the army?"

Kendal predicted Yoodle would go ballistic when her main attack failed.

At the right time, Kendal intended to step up and act as a decoy. He'd irritate Yoodle by buzzing in her ear, loud enough to make her go nuts. With a head start, he planned to outrace her to the secondary target.

"With your permission, Queen Victoria," Kendal said. "I'll lead the killer bees to your front door."

Two queens balked; they were offended killer bees were invited to their front door. Queen Victoria asked them to settle down. She asked Kendal the question eating at everyone's mind. "What's the role for queens in the strategy?"

"Did you ever see yourselves as bait for the enemy?" Kendal asked. Here's your opportunity to perform in a drama involving life and death."

Kendal instructed the queens to act frightened; the more scared they appeared the better. That gives the lieutenants a false sense of confidence. Slam the entrance door behind the lieutenants, trapping them between the hive entrance and the Council hall.

Kendal knew the queens were fit for the job. Physically, they were well armed to defend themselves. Their skins were thick as leather. They were able to sting repeatedly as only queen bees can do. In addition, they possessed the power of royal longevity ... insurance to live a thousand years. Without exception, the Queen's Council approved Kendal's plan.

The responsibility to confront Yoodle belonged to Zoey. She

asked Mame and Dame to act as her seconds, to offset two bodyguards Yoodle employed. Zoey figured three against three was fair.

Dame and Mame were ready to climb into the ring with
Yoodle's heavyweight guards. They even offered to teach Zoey a
new wrestling hold to use on Yoodle. They said there was time to
limber up and to practice.

Victoria congratulated Kendal and Zoey. For a diversion a
special event was planned to honor Zoey. No sooner had the queens
filed out of the hall than the bell promptly recalled them. Show
time! A fashion parade began, dedicated in Zoey's honor.

In small groups, the queens gathered like cheerleaders to
support the contestant of their choice. Though the hall was dark,
the stage was lit up in rich luminous colors ... greens, blues, oranges
and of course white, the favorite color of bees. A portable runway
branched out from the stage; it allowed each queen to promenade
deep into the audience, attired in her high fashion outfit.

Queen Victoria, adorned in a gold robe, came forward to act
as the mistress of ceremonies.

"Welcome to our First Annual Queens' Fashion Show. I'm
proud to introduce the eight competitors in search for the title,
'Beauty Queen for the Year.' Without further adieu, our first contestant is Leah, modeling a modern motif—

"Look at Grandma, Mother. She struts like a professional
model," Kendal quipped. "She sways as she skips along. See how
she stares at the audience to keep their attention."

"—her hair coiffure is stiffened to stand straight up; Queen
Leah has chosen designer jeans with appropriate rips and mend-
ing, and a blouse of emerald green."

Queen Leah promenaded along the runway with finesse. She
watched her step, careful not to trip. To maintain grace and balance while wearing flip flop shoes required her attention. Leah
reached the stage safely. As she bowed and exited, she acknowledged the applause.

Following Leah, Queen Victoria introduced each contestant,

one by one … adorned in gowns, gloves, headgear, and hoops, with one queen wearing two tone shaded sun glasses.

Mame and Dame made their debut with a splash. With their colorful wrestling outfits, T-shirts and matching pants, they back flipped along the runway, in time with the beat of the applause.

Following their act, Queen Martha glided across the stage in a white silky gown with matching white bonnet speckled with blue sequins. Martha knew how to captivate the audience … to enter, pose and exit with style and stage presence. And the winner was—

After taking her bows, Queen Martha asked for attention. "I believe Kendal should play a part. He's the only drone attending the festivities. Don't you agree, ladies?" They all whooped it up as teenagers at a rock concert.

"I don't want to embarrass you, Kendal … Please sing us a song?" Martha asked.

Kendal never performed in front of an audience. His songs were reserved for the bakery shop. There, Kendal and Greeney practiced duets or harmonized humming. But Kendal nodded O.K. He moved center stage, caught the right note on the tip of his tongue and delivered in a baritone voice. The queens listened in silence; they never heard the song before … an original Kendal composition, entitled 'Greeney and Me.' The retirees thought the lyrics were marvelous. After a few stanzas, the queens joined in the refrain.

After the show, the queens retired, tired after a trying day. Zoey joined Mame and Dame to practice wrestling holds. Kendal approached the entrance, now staffed with four guards. He peered out at the world he learned to love. Tomorrow was another story. Ready or not, he must rest before encountering the killer bees.

# Chapter Eighteen

# Going Into Action

No queen needed an alarm clock. Before the birds twittered, all 304 queens wandered the halls; six of them knocked over this and that. Their nerves were frayed; the killer bees weren't far away.

In the dining room, most tables were occupied. Queens wiled away the time, drinking honey tea. They chatted nervously.

Balancing on the limb outside the hive, Zoey practiced her wrestling holds under the watchful supervision of Mame and Dame. In final preparation, they tightened their black belts around their abdomens.

In Victoria's chamber, Kendal discussed last minute defense strategies with Victoria, Leah and Zoey. As they finished, Kendal leaned over to kiss each of the queens on the cheek. Off he jetted to establish a front line position near Zoey's hive.

In thick bushes, Kendal rearranged some milkweed leaves and covered his body. The foul smelling foliage would discourage anyone from exploring the bush, except a stray caterpillar. His presence should go undetected.

*** 

Sleeping on Aidan's bed, Heydog poked him with his wet nose. He whined, pretending he needed to go outside to pee. He scratched at the pillow until Aidan slid off the bed. The cold floor made no impression on Aidan as he fumbled his way through the kitchen. The wise canary heard them. He called to his beagle friend. "You're up to foolish stuff again, Heydog. I can tell by the way you're hurrying."

"Shut your bird trap, little friend. Go back to sleep."

With the door barely open, Heydog squeezed by Aidan. He glided into the darkness. In a half daze, Aidan rushed back to bed confident that Heydog was capable of surviving outdoors till morning. But the beagle had other ideas.

Heydog ran through the forest aiming at a spot south of Zoey's hive. There he crawled on all fours through misty coated bushes. A loud buzzing blared only ten feet away. Darn! There they were— the killer bee swarm roosted high in a maple tree buzzing in agitation. Heydog heard a commotion … the buzzing grew louder. The killer bees were in a frenzy. As careful as he tried to be silent Heydog was detected. Trouble was on the way.

One alert scout heard the snap of a branch. The scout released a warning scent through the swarm. The odor indicated a present danger.

The hyper killer bees wasted no time. In gangs they erupted from the swarm to chase Heydog. He howled 'ArRoooo' … 'ArRoooo.' … The beagle warning gave Kendal notice the killer bees were sighted. Off Heydog scurried as he tried to outrun the killers in hot pursuit.

In battle formation, six squads caught Heydog in an open field. The first sting hurt the worse. Repeatedly, they struck with pin point accuracy—over and over. Soon Heydog resembled a black glob of oil. Down he fell. Not a muscle fluttered. After so many stings, Heydog dropped, not moving even his long ears.

Losing so many of her bees didn't bother Yoodle; her face kept its blank stare. As long as they defeated the enemy, she considered the operation a success. Her attention fixed on her target; her face turned flush red with anticipation.

"Advance," she ordered. "It's time to show Zoey who's the strongest queen."

Under the lieutenants' directions, Yoodle's bees rallied. In attack formation, they murmured the same sounds as a buzz saw. Without another command, they moved as one body toward their target. In no time they traveled north to Zoey's hive, with Yoodle and the lieutenants trailing safely behind.

The attacking army followed orders. In continuous waves, they raced into the hive … a gang of them flew upstairs, others darted downstairs; the rest flew around the inside of the great hall. They occupied every imaginable space, even empty cells in the honey combs. When they landed on any surface, the killer bees became stuck. If one stopped to help another, she found herself stuck too. In no time no one was able to budge, to take one step.

From his vantage point in the milkweed bush, Kendal knew Yoodle's bees inside the hive were out of action. The loud buzzing diminished to a whimper, hardly the noise of a conquering army. A few cries for help seeped out of the hive. Not one bee escaped.

Kendal uncovered the camouflaged leaves and made his move on Yoodle's position. "Catch me if you can," he yelled as he buzzed close to Yoodle's head, trying to antagonize her. Yoodle forgot about her main army when she recognized the bee wearing the white fluffy hat. No doubt at all, this was Kendal.

"After him," Yoodle yelled. Her lieutenants took off to chase Kendal.

Hardly outracing the lieutenants, Kendal neared the old oak tree hive entrance. *Oh no,* he thought. An old queen lay on her stomach, on top of the limb. Kendal recognized her … number 2 was prone to falling. As she struggled toward the hive entrance, number 2 had fallen on her face. Kendal didn't hesitate. He swooped down and helped her gain her legs; she scampered safely through the entrance.

While Kendal was lending a hand, a squad of lieutenants arrived, too late to detain queen number 2. They landed in the nick of time to block Kendal from escaping. "Stay right where you are," the leader commanded. "Let's see what our Queen wants to do with you."

Kendal surrendered. He had no choice with six dangerous lieutenants poised to sting him. Yoodle pushed the lieutenants aside as she docked on the limb. Capturing her enemy with the white fluffy hat made her day. "One down!" she exclaimed … "My next target is Zoey."

Yoodle ordered Louisi to select two lieutenants for guard duty. They were ordered to take Kendal into custody and wait at the bottom of the tree until she called for them. If the drone tried to escape, the lieutenants were ordered to sting him with a mild dose. Yoodle wanted the pleasure of settling with Kendal after the lieutenants captured Zoey.

Yoodle's elite lieutenants gathered about her. "Organize into squads," she ordered. "On my command, rush the hive. Once inside, there's a hallway connecting with the Queens' meeting room. The old queens will be cringing there for safety, I'm sure. Show no mercy. Kill them all. I'll wait for the all clear signal. Do it. Go."

Without hesitation, the lieutenants stormed the hive entrance. As they cleared the doorway, a spring lock gave way. The heavy door suspended from the ceiling hit the ground with a thud. The lieutenants were sealed inside.

There was only one direction for them to go—straight ahead. Four abreast in tight formation, the lieutenants advanced. They marched double time, stopping only as they reached the Council's meeting room door. When a siren blared, the large oak door swung open.

A solid line of bearded queens pretended to be afraid. The ladies weren't intimidated. Staring straight into the lieutenants' eyes, an ancient looking queen challenged them. "How dare you bitter bees enter our home with murder in your hearts?"

"Attack," a lieutenant commanded. "Kill the queens, go, go ... "

As the lieutenant rushed into battle, the queen's front line broke in its center. The lieutenants ran into empty air. The queens realigned themselves along the walls. They waited patiently until all the lieutenants were tucked inside the room.

"Close ranks behind them," boomed Victoria. "Good going, my sisters. We trapped them all."

The lieutenants were no match for the bearded old queens with leather skins and sharpened stingers.

Outside, at the base of the old oak tree, Kendal was held prisoner by Louisi and her two conspirators. They racked their brains on a way to escape Yoodle's influence. Kendal heard them complaining. But he had a more pressing concern, how to aid the old queens fighting for their lives inside. They might need him. How— He looked twice when a lieutenant spoke to him with civility. "Aren't you Tee's friend, Kendal?" Louisi inquired.

"Yes, that's me," he replied. "How do you know my name?"

"Tee and I were cell mates in a dungeon a few days ago. He told me your name." Louisi recalled Tee's kindness and a description of the princely Kendal. She hoped one day to live with that kind of bee.

"I heard you three conspirators talking," Kendal said bluntly. "If you really want to free yourselves from Yoodle's yoke, you can do it."

"Can you help us, Kendal?" Louisi asked.

"The three of you?"

"Yes, the three of us want freedom."

Kendal agreed. He led them to the rear entrance. He rapped three times on the door. A queen in battle regalia recognized Kendal and let them in. Kendal said the lieutenants were friends. They were on their way to find Victoria.

When they arrived upstairs, only killer bee bodies were strewn over the floor. Weary, exhausted queens checked pulses to see if any one survived. The queens didn't want anyone to suffer.

As Kendal searched for his mother, he spotted Queen Victoria supervising clean up operations. Kendal rushed to her side. No where did he see Zoey in this chaotic battle scene. Visibly stewing about Zoey's safety, he asked, "Queen Victoria, where's my mother?"

"Zoey's safe, Kendal. She's out on the limb, preparing to engage Queen Yoodel."

"I'd better hurry. I want to help her. These three lieutenants seek a safe haven to start a new life. Can you help them, Queen Victoria?"

"Of course, Kendal. You go and join your mother. She needs you."

# Chapter Nineteen

# Two Queens Do Battle

Kendal dashed down the hallway, looking for Zoey. At the hive entrance she stood, readying for the battle of her life. Mame and Dame were stationed faithfully at her side attired for battle as her seconds. Each wore their distinctive badges ... Mame 108 ... Dame 188 ... Queen Zoey wore a new number, 304. Those numbers were to be etched in Kendal's head for evermore.

Kendal wished he could take his mother's place. But it was her right as queen to engage Yoodle. He knew his fighting skills were blah at best. When Zoey spotted him, she waited for a kiss for good luck. Then she marched bravely out on the limb, Mame and Dame on either side.

"Where are you hiding, Yoodle?" Queen Zoey challenged her enemy. "We have serious business—you and I. Come out and stand up on your own six feet."

Kendal never heard his mother raise her voice before, even when she briefed forty thousand bees each morning. Zoey always spoke gently as you do when you're making conversation with friends.

Yoodle didn't reply. She had no time to waste in small talk. She stomped down on one of her bodyguard's feet. "It's time to fight, no more talk," she dictated. She waited in her hole. Where were her lieutenants? They always reported to her promptly. Yoodle was confident of total victory.

The lieutenants had been coached before the attack, to jump on Zoey and hold her down. Yoodle then would administer two or three stings, maybe more. Painful barbs can rip the skin … who cared? *The more the better*, Yoodle thought.—"Ugh!" Yoodle grabbed at her stomach as she burped loud and clear. *Must have been something I ate,* she thought; her stomach rumbled, gurgling uncontrollably.

"Yoodle," Zoey raised her voice a decibel or two. "Your entire company of lieutenants is gone. It's you and me. You made the decision to war on us. My two queen sisters are here with me. We're ready to fight—three against three. I'm offering you a fair fight."

And still Yoodle waited; she took her own sweet time to edge out of a crack in the bark. She peeked over the lid. So this was the great and kind queen that Tee bragged about. Shrilly, she laughed herself silly.

"Look, bodyguards—our so called enemies … this is pathetic—three tired old queens. Two wearing long silvery beards; one has a new goatee. The two with beards are so ancient they fastened black belts around their stomachs to hold their beards in place. We'll kill them all," she said in a threatening rage.

Queen Yoodle hopped out of the crack, ready to do battle. She played the part of the great warrior, ready to pounce on her enemy. Her two bodyguards crawled behind her.

As the combatants closed on each other, Yoodle tricked Zoey as she faked a lunge. Zoey wasn't fooled. Kendal called out encouragement.

Zoey countered with a right jab of her forearm.

Yoodle's bodyguards tried to defend themselves. Muscle bound bodyguards were no match against Mame and Dame.

Out of breath, Zoey offered Yoodle one last chance to give up. Her colony of retirees was prepared to assist even a queen requiring rehabilitation.

"Yoodle," Queen Zoey challenged her once more. "Your army is stuck fast in my hive with resin and your lieutenants are all dead. Give yourself up."

The ultimatum infuriated Yoodle. Her face lit up brighter than a one hundred watt scarlet red bulb. She advanced, blindly. Zoey sidestepped, tripping Yoodle who somersaulted, hitting the ground with a resounding thump.

"Watch out for tricks, Mother," Kendal warned.

Enough was enough … time to use the wrestling trick she practiced—the Lazy Susan Slam. Zoey grabbed hold of Yoodle's wing and flipped her over on her back. With the spring of youth, Zoey landed on top. That did it. She didn't have time to think; she stung her enemy where it hurt, penetrating the same spot, over and over again.

Kendal hurried out on the limb to embrace Zoey. "Mother, are you all right?" he asked.

"Perfectly fine, Kendal. It has been an interesting day, hasn't it?" Then she collapsed on her rear end to rest.

Victoria and Leah lost no time to bustle out of the hive to check on Zoey and the champion tag team. They were no worse for wear after the head to head fight with the bodyguards.

Kendal heard a familiar noise. Aidan's wagon rattled as it bumped along. Aidan called, *"Whoa."* He stopped the wagon directly beneath the oak tree limb. Looking up, Aidan saw the queens and his pal drone. Kendal flew down to sit on Aidan's knee.

Aidan in short spurts spieled off why he came this morning … he woke up … searched for Heydog … remembered … he didn't leave him back indoors … Aidan thought he came this way … he ran to his mother … she let him borrow the wagon … he came to find Heydog. Aidan spouted off one concern after another. Kendal wished he might lighten Aidan's heavy heart.

Heydog was a worry. The beagle's 'ArRoooo' had blared out a plea for mercy. The sound meant he faced deep trouble when he signaled Kendal that the killer bees were on the march.

When Aidan noticed the frown on the drone's face, he shared his good news. Kendal's family arrived at his house in a swarm, late yesterday afternoon. The bees took up residency in the vacant hive right outside Aidan's bedroom. He said he watched closely as the colony settled in. The worker bees lost no time in finding pollen and nectar. He even spotted the new young queen.

Queen Zoey bounced and settled on Aidan's other knee. She cracked her first smile after the stress of fighting Yoodle. Aidan's news raised Kendal's spirit to know Zoey's colony was established in a new hive. Aidan shared other news, how his family found a large supply of honey on the ground. His mother estimated it exceeded a thousand pounds.

A weak 'ArRooo' sounded through the trees, followed by a fainter 'ArRoo.' Aidan knew the voice. Heydog's baying couldn't fool anyone. "I've gotta go," Aidan said.

Kendal made no effort to fly off Aidan's knee as Zoey flew away.

"Get up, Mosey," Aidan yelled. Mosey almost galloped ahead. He tracked Heydog's moans without anymore encouragement.

Aidan glimpsed Heydog limping out from thick spruce trees. His body was one black mess, covered with barbs. Even his nose and cheeks rippled with scattered stingers.

"*Whoa,*" Aidan ordered. He jumped off the wagon as Kendal hovered over his shoulder. Sobbing, Aidan rushed to check Heydog's injuries.

"I'll take you right home, buddy," Aidan told Heydog. "Mom has tweezers and antiseptic for those stingers." He lost no time. Climbing on the wagon, Aidan waved to Kendal and hurried home.

Back on the old oak tree limb, Kendal reported his news. He worried about Aidan who drove alone with a wounded animal.

Mame and Dame volunteered to follow Aidan in case he needed help. They also agreed to deliver a message to Tee to send back drones to help Kendal.

Before Aidan traveled a mile, Mame and Dame caught up with the wagon. They landed on the seat next to Aidan. There they sat quietly to prove their best intentions. Aidan welcomed the company.

Mrs. Bright heard the rattling of the wagon approaching the house. She ran outdoors with Kim. They helped carry the poor beagle into the kitchen. An open front door was an invitation for Mame and Dame to join the family as they performed first aid. Because the queens possessed a keen sense of smell, they examined the beagle's body. They hovered over deep stingers. Mrs. Bright appreciated their pointers.

After emergency medical attention, Mame and Dame searched outdoors for Tee to deliver a message. Kendal asked Tee to send him help to set up a new bakery.

Kendal's mind raced one hundred miles an hour. He thought about Tee and Handy and the whole bakery crew ... poor Greeney in her cocoon ... the two new caterpillars Greeney recruited ... the killer bees stuck in resin ... and now Heydog's need to heal. What to do first? A sticky question for Kendal to decide.

# Chapter Twenty

# Unfinished Business

When too many problems weighed Kendal down, he tried to apply a simple rule … first things, first. At this moment, thousands of defenseless, misguided bees were trapped in a resin jam. They deserved first priority on Kendal's list. He told Zoey he must go help the stuck killer bees. She agreed his decision was the right one. The emergency Council meeting called by Victoria could wait.

Flying directly to Zoey's hive, Kendal carefully approached the entrance. He peered inside. "What a mess!" he exclaimed loudly as he saw the contorted bodies filling every space. Wherever Kendal gazed, killer bees were stuck, fastened on the floor, on the walls and fixed to the ceilings. Workers were glued to each other—wings fastened together, heads attached, legs entangled and even antennae bound. Yoodle's worker bees clogged the surfaces as thick as a sewer back up.

A few frantic bees strained to free themselves without success. Kendal must do something, somehow. But—there were a number of choices: leave them the way they were ... smoke them good ... forget them ... forgive them for their misdeeds and try to render assistance.

Gingerly, Kendal advanced three tiny steps. Any contact with resin sealed his fate if he weren't careful. His drones proved how efficient they were as a gang of painters; they didn't miss one spot when applying the resin. He called out to no one in particular, faces were hard to see. "My name's Kendal. You've got yourselves in one awful situation here."

From every quarter of the hive, Kendal heard cries and moans, frustration exploding in earnest. "Help me ... help me ... unstick me. ... " In one thunderous roar the pleas resounded, "Help ... Help ... Help" in a cadence count. One piercing voice rose above the din, a voice to quiet all the others. This was the voice of a popular killer bee, one of the few respected by the others.

"Can we discuss our situation?" the voice asked.

"Of course," Kendal replied. "That's why I'm here."

"We concede we lost the battle," the voice said. "We're permanently stuck unless you help. Without question, our attitudes are aggressive because we were trained to fight, rather than to love. It's the way Queen Yoodle fostered the spirit of our colony. And our lieutenants enforced Yoodle's rules of terror. Do you know what I'm saying?"

"I hear you," Kendal replied. "And do you understand the dilemma, I'm facing?"

"Yes, I surely do," the voice asserted. She admitted she didn't know how she'd act if she were in Kendal's shoes. The voice confessed they were wrong. They were sorry to be part of Yoodle's conquering army. They yearned to be useful citizens in a peaceful colony. They offered their energy and experience. With a chance, they might become bees of good will.

From the direction of the voice, Kendal identified the spokesbee. She looked sincere even stuck upside down.

"I'll offer you a deal if you promise to behave," Kendal said. "A pardon for good deeds. Release for good behavior, for everyone caught in the resin."

"I'm sure all of us stuck here will agree to your terms. But if you release us, we don't have a queen bee, no one to lay eggs to produce a larger colony."

"I believe I can resolve that problem," Kendal responded. "It's a practical solution."

Kendal suggested the voice canvass her colleagues who were trapped in the hive. She must obtain their agreement to abide by rules of kindness and good beeship. Kendal was willing to trust the voice to conduct an impartial vote. While they consulted among themselves, he waited patiently. But timing was important in his plan.

The voice spread the word to a few bees near by. Soon, their whispers and murmurs replaced the whining. With a resounding, Yes … Yes … Yes, they agreed. They were prepared to learn new ways. The lead voice assured Kendal of agreement among all the workers to change their lives around.

"So be it," Kendal responded. "I'm glad. Let's take the first step toward freedom." He explained what he had in mind. A clean up crew of his drone friends was on the way here. By tapping into a reserve supply of detergent, the resin could be dissolved easily. The drones were experts with hoses. They knew how to aim for the best results. They'd wash down the nearest stuck bees. In turn the freed killer bees were to cleanse others covered by the resin. Then over and over, repeating the procedure until everyone was free from the sticky resin.

Kendal guaranteed his drones knew how to deliver the necessary detergent wherever the bees were stuck. They were all transportation specialists after successfully moving mountains of honey bee cylinders to the ground. If the killer worker bees kept their cool, Kendal pledged to return shortly, bringing fresh ideas to restart their colony.

Fortunately, when Kendal arrived at the old oak tree he was able to get a message to his mother who was secluded behind closed doors. She was now a full fledged member of the Council, and an emergency session was in progress. After Zoey received the message of urgency, she excused herself and ran to Kendal. He described his proposal to help the killer bees and she agreed.

By the time Kendal shuttled back to the trapped bees, he found them drying off, the resin washed away. All the killer bees stood around asking each other, what was in store for them.

Kendal called for a meeting with their representatives. Fifty killer bee workers gathered around him. Kendal invited killer bees to designate two of their own drones to join the discussion. As they positioned themselves at the bakery table in Zoey's basement, Kendal identified their basic need, a full functioning hive with honey inventory to get them going. He had the answer. Queen Zoey gifted her hive to them as their new home with all of its honey supply.

"That's unbelievable," one of the representatives said ... Kendal detected the same familiar voice speaking. "How generous of Queen Zoey! You mean this bakery and the cafeteria too. That's—"

Kendal continued, "Whatever you find in the hive belongs to your colony." There was no way a colony survived without a queen bee. So he made arrangements for a queen to lay eggs. Queen Zoey, recently retired, scheduled her time to return as their temporary queen, for a day or two. Laying eggs was her specialty. With more worker bees hatched, their colony might double and triple soon. One of her fertilized eggs could become the 'kind bees' queen as part of Kendal's relief plan.

"You're serious?" one familiar voice chimed in, the voice cracking. "This queen that we attacked, *(sobbing)* is willing to help us rebuild our colony?"

"Yes, I'm serious," Kendal answered. "That's our way." But there were two conditions in order to finalize the arrangement— because many killer bees were taught to practice bad social habits,

Queen Martha offered to give lessons in etiquette and good manners to the killer bees. In addition, killer bee drones will attend baking lessons to be taught by Kendal's drones assigned on temporary duty. And so, Kendal rested his proposal.

Kendal's plan answered the worker bees' dreams—a basketful of benefits, the best news the killer bees ever heard. No one ever treated them with such kindness. Without warning, four husky ladies hoisted Kendal high on their shoulders. They paraded him about for all to see and cheer. As they set Kendal down, without further fanfare he waved goodbye. Other unfinished business required his attention.

# Chapter Twenty-One

# Royal Shocker

Behind the Council's doors, a bedlam rocked the meeting hall. The queens ran around, arguing and bickering about this and that. Queen Victoria tried to control the queens. She called for order in a stern voice. "Quiet down. Take your places." She tried again and again to get order using a voice two octaves higher than normal.

"Dear sisters ... ladies ... please ... take your seats ... thanks, my dears. It's good for us to be here, safe and sound. The danger is over; thanks to Zoey, Kendal, and his drones. Let's not forget our part in the victory. Each of us played a key role in defeating the killer bees."

Without waiting for the other queens, Victoria flapped her wings ... in unison, the others joined in, to applaud their colony of 304 retired queens.

Once the applause started, Queen Martha slipped out the door. As the queens calmed down, Martha returned. She moved to Victoria's side carrying a box tied with a royal blue ribbon. She pulled the end of the knot and opened the box ... displaying the contents to Victoria.

"Do you agree, Victoria?" Martha asked as she revealed the contents to Victoria. "Absolutely, Martha," Queen Victoria replied.

Queen Martha extracted two items from the box. She held them high for all to see. The reactions were vocal and instantaneous: "Ah, Ah … gosh … wow … ohhh … right on!" The exclamations exploded like fireworks displays. The two items Martha held over her head conveyed the same message to each of the queens.

Queen Victoria asked Zoey to go find Kendall and ask him to appear before the Council at 4:00 p.m. "Zoey, please keep Kendal in suspense until we meet, won't you?" Victoria urged. Zoey agreed. No one cared to spoil Kendal's surprise for anything.

Martha supervised the arrangements. Her reputation to organize exceeded even her accomplishments in the kitchen. Martha assigned queens to various committees for this, for that, and for the other thing. As the queens left the Council hall, it was evident their competitive spirit was restored. They scampered out to make appointments at the beauty shop before 4:00 p.m.

As the queens charged out of the hall, Zoey and Leah sat down with Victoria to discuss a favorite subject, "Kendal." As parents and grandparents do without being asked, Zoey and Leah started to boast about their son and grandson. Nothing else bonded the three queens more than their interests in Kendal. Each claimed some responsibility for molding him as a masterpiece in motion.

"Well, as far as I'm concerned," Leah remarked. "Kendal has earned his rightful place in our long line of queens possessing royal longevity. Male though he be, Kendal is the last bee in the royal line."

"Dear ladies, I'm not sure Kendal is the end of the royal line," Zoey said. "I can't tell you why—that's what my heart tells me."

At 4:00 p.m. promptly, the queens assembled. Kendal fidgeted outside, waiting to be summoned. His first order of business was to compliment the retirees for their part in the victory over the killer bees. The queens deserved praise and gratitude. That was Kendal's agenda. The queens' agenda was quite different.

Zoey opened the door, smacking her lips to keep them locked. She beckoned Kendal to join her. He was startled. The retirees were clean shaven except Victoria. Her beard was thinned and shaped in a V form. Each queen wore a white coiffure hairdo, styled with early American curls dangling loosely over her eyes.

"Is this another fashion show?" Kendal asked. "What's the occasion?"

"Come and see, Kendal," Victoria responded eagerly. "Join me at the podium."

Victoria turned to Kendal as she read off his accomplishments over the last few days. She thanked him on behalf of the grateful assembly in a solemn voice. Victoria then declared, "After careful consideration and unanimous agreement, without dissent or question, for the first time in my memory, and it's a long one, the royal queens of Virginia, set precedent in the world of bees."

*What nonsense is this?* Kendal was puzzled. *What did Queen Victoria mean by all this formal flowery language?*

"Kendal, please kneel before me." Queen Victoria said.

Thoroughly confused, Kendal knelt down on his left legs. He held his shoulders back, his back straight and his head high. *What a crazy ritual. What was going on here?*

Queen Martha handed a silver wand to Victoria. She waved the wand in circular motions over Kendal's head, three times. She lowered the wand on Kendal's shoulder as she pronounced the words distinctly, "Hail, Hail Kendal, First King of the Bees."

The queens refrained from shouting out. Victoria removed the first of two items from Martha's box. Carefully she unfolded an emerald green cape with the monogram KB blazoned in gold. She draped it over Kendal's back, fastening it under his chin with a beespeckled latch. Next, she lifted out a gold crown, crafted to be worn by a drone whose eyes stood on top of his head. "Wear this crown proudly, King Kendal, with justifiable pride for all your kind deeds and marvelous achievements."

No longer could the queens be silent. The room erupted in deafening cheers. Vibrations caused a tall honeycomb to fall over. They all shouted. "Hail ... Hail, King of the Bees."

Zoey wiped tears out of her eyes as she spoke a few words. First, she acknowledged the special qualities Kendal exemplified from the beginning. Although he was born last in the line of royal succession, Kendal attained many firsts for drones. She listed them: First to attend school, to master a trade, to get a job, to make friends with people, to teach a trade, and to employ a caterpillar. If that wasn't enough firsts, he saved Zoey, distributed miracle cakes, designed a defense strategy and earned the 'Hero of the Hive' citation.

The queens let Zoey's words ring in their ears. Queen Victoria pondered on Zoey's message too. There was nothing for her to add. If any of the retirees wanted more personal information about Kendal, Victoria referred them to his mother or grandmother. Either one was quite willing to talk about Kendal, any time.

With the ceremony concluded, Queen Victoria announced. "Let the festivities begin."

In anticipation of a special occasion, Martha prepared all kinds of delicacies. They were locked away waiting for a major event to come along. Thousands of fancy goodies were made using Martha's blue ribbon recipes. Victoria asked for three volunteers to serve the treats. Thirty-one queens ran to Martha's side.

Kendal coughed to get attention. He wished to be heard. "My dear ladies, you do me the greatest of honor as a drone. Now, I have places to go and work to do. Queen Zoey has agreed to act as substitute queen for the killer bees. They really prefer a different name. They'd like to be called KB which stands for 'kind bees' in the future. Since their colony has agreed to reform, they will need a new queen and a few drones. Zoey says she can spare a few eggs to help them."

"Doesn't Kendal have a fine sense of humor," queen number 2 quipped. They all laughed when they heard Zoey was anxious to return to work. Number 2 was sharp as usual. She reminded her sisters, 'KB' stood not only for 'kind bees' but also 'King of the Bees.'

Kendal bowed to queen number 2. He wished to make a few announcements. The 'kind bees' agreed to learn etiquette from Queen Martha. The resin clean up in Zoey's hive was completed. Tee was loaning the time of a few baker bees to teach the 'kind bees' until their drones learned the baker trade.—

A persistent tapping sounded on the Council door. As Martha opened it, she backed off in shock. There stood two caterpillars thoroughly confused, as confused as Martha. The caterpillars told her they agreed to replace Greeney in the hive—to report at the old oak tree.

Kendal apologized for the change in plans. Their services were in dire need elsewhere. Kendal asked if they were willing to turn around and return to Queen Zoey's hive. A young colony of 'kind bees' needed their help. Why not, they had nothing better to do. Thanking them, Kendal suggested the caterpillars enjoy refreshments before making the long trek back to where they started.

Kendal asked a favor of Queen Victoria. Could she inform the local queens that Aidan's family thanked them for their honey contributions? All together, 1,000 pounds of honey was collected. Queen Leah said she'd prepare a thank you note.

Kendal checked his list of unfinished business. Not a long list anymore. However, one urgent item needed attention.

Chapter Twenty-Two

# Share The Good News

When 304 queens gathered for a celebration, it soon became a royal racket. They had decorated the Council hall from top to bottom … pendants and banners on the walls. The coronation of the First King of the Bees was topic of the day as they all gathered in clusters to laugh and even cry. What fun!

Kendal slipped to Zoey's side without anyone noticing.

"Mother, I'm going to skip the festivities if you don't mind. I'm glad to see the queens enjoying the party. They deserve some fun after what they've been through. … I'll be back before dark."

In her role as a caring mother, she asked, "Where are you going, Kendal?"

"I'm going to Aidan's house. I'll check on Tee and the drones. My honors are too good to hide from them. Without their hard work and initiative, this day wasn't possible."

Kendal stowed away his crown and cape in his back pack. The two mile flight to Aidan's home was easy for a powerful flyer. As he winged northward, Kendal started to cross the field where 140 hives surrounded Aidan's home. Kendal proceeded with care. Angry scouts hounded him on the last two trips here. Today, Kendal preferred a peaceful flight.

Oh, oh, the scouts were out in force today. Outside every hive, they loitered, and then they came to attention. They looked up and saluted Kendal. *That's strange behavior,* he thought.

Great … Aidan and Kim were seated on the porch; Heydog slept on a blanket near them. Kendal did a four point landing on the boy's knee. Aidan almost knocked Kendal to the floor as he jumped up. He was glad to see his drone pal and thank him for the help of the two queen bees to make Heydog well.

"Oh look—Heydog's opening one eye," yelled Aidan.

Kendal flew to Heydog, landing on his paw. "Hey, buddy, you were a great help. And you were so brave. How are you doing?"

"A bit groggy, but I'm on the mend. The two queens you sent introduced themselves. They were quick on their feet."

Heydog scratched at the air as he did when digging a hole in the dirt. Aidan understood his best friend. He was hungry. A healthy sign!

Kendal stroked Heydog's paw and thanked him for the alert when the killer bees were on the way to attack Zoey's hive. The 'ArRoooo' worked as a bugle call, to prepare Kendal for the invasion. He described the coronation ceremony and told Heydog about his cape and crown.

"I'd love to see them," Heyday pleaded.

"They're in my back pack."

"C'mon Kendal, put them on, please."

Kendal undid the flap. He removed the cape and flipped it over his shoulders. He tied it under his chin. He learned how to tie knots as a larva when he spun his cocoon ages ago. Next he removed the crown and placed it on his head.

"Wow! You'll wow the ladies in that outfit, Kendal."

Aidan happened to return with biscuits. Plop. The box dropped from his hands, almost hitting Heydog on the nose. He flinched and snatched a loose biscuit. The drone was dressed in a king's robe and crown. As Aidan rubbed his eyes in disbelief, he heard the rattling wagon. Mrs. Bright was returning from shopping. He jumped off the stoop to grab his mother's hand, insisting she follow him.

"Come quickly, Mom. You have to see this to believe it."

Mrs. Bright studied Kendal in his royal garb. "You're right, Aidan. I wouldn't believe this if I didn't see it with my own eyes. A drone dressed up in a king's outfit. Is this scene for real?"

Mrs. Bright couldn't wait to share her news … How her friend, a professor, completed the analysis of the miracle cake samples. These were the same ingots Kendal left on the kitchen table. The professor arranged for the miracle cakes to be marketed wherever beekeepers cared for colonies of honey bees.

Kendal did a dance in delight. Awesome news! But there was more good news to tell. Mrs. Bright heard an announcement on the radio, rain was on the way. Starting in the morning, a drenching rain was coming as displayed on Doppler radar.

"My gosh!" Kendal exclaimed to himself. The queens and every bee were anxious for cool air to help them air condition their hives.

Mrs. Bright caught her own giggle, but she was so excited. She asked Aidan to detain his little drone friend for another minute. She had an idea.

Hurrying out of the room, Mrs. Bright returned with her digital camera. She asked Aidan and Kim to sit on either side of Heydog who held Kendal on one paw. If she snapped the right picture, it might be used on the cake packaging for marketing the new miracle cakes product. In that way, the little drone might receive credit for discovering the recipe. He deserved recognition.

So far, Kim hardly said a word as she watched. But she too was fascinated with bees and everything in nature. She learned to love creatures from her favorite people, the American Indians.

Their writings were filled with stories of clouds, trees, rocks, the sun and moon and of course the animals and the bees. Kim snatched a book off the porch table to read one special sentiment expressed by a chief of the Lakota tribe. When thinking about death, the American Indian wrote:

> *Oh, Great Spirit, whose voice I hear in the winds*
> *Whose breath gives life to the world, hear me*
> *I come to you as one of your many children*
> *I am small and weak*
> *I need your strength and wisdom*
> —attr. Chief Yellow Lark, 1887

That Lakota message spoke directly to Kendal's heart. These words expressed the way he was thinking as he plodded through the passage of nature's ways.

Speaking about ways, he'd best be on his way. Kendal wished Heydog a rapid recovery. He waved to Aidan, Kim and their mother. Wearing his crown and cape proudly, Kendal flew from the porch and around the house. He had no trouble finding the right hive. Tee, Handy and Rebecca stood outside the entrance welcoming Kendal with yellow bits of yarn.

Rebecca invited him inside. "Kendal, we saw you arrive at the house. Congratulations. I heard about your coronation … you were declared 'First King of the Bees.' I think that's splendid."

"Yes, Rebecca. The queens bestowed the title on me. I wanted to share the news with you, my family."

"That's us," Tee reacted. "Me too," Handy declared with gusto.

"Follow us downstairs," Tee urged as he led the way. "There's a small reception set up in the cafeteria."

As they entered, Mia was lounging on a bench, nibbling on pastries served by four attentive drones. Already, she was popular with the guys. Rebecca introduced Kendal who had never met Mia formally.

"Hello, Mia," Kendal said, appreciating that Mia made a fine impression as a new queen.

"Hi Kendal," Mia replied. "What's that you're wearing?" she asked.

"They're gifts from the queens in the old oak tree hive. You've met my mother, haven't you, Mia?"

"I met Queen Zoey only once. She treated me well. Do all queens in retirement live in harmony?"

"Absolutely. They're having the time of their lives, no responsibilities, no laying eggs for them. The queens were celebrating when I left them earlier today."

"Well, I'll be starting my queen's duties too. As soon as I mate, I'll lay eggs. Until then, I'm enjoying my leisure time with worker bees and drones chasing me all over the hive … this is fun and games."

"Tee," Kendal said in a bewildering tone, "Is that who I think it is at the table … reading books?"

"Oh yes! Jockie. Bookie encouraged him to learn to read."

Jockie saw Kendal and struggled to rise to his feet.

"What's wrong?" Kendal asked.

"Jockie is using a walker that Mechie made. Our athlete sprained his leg when we were applying the resin. He can fly, but he can't put much weight on his feet."

"Well, Tee," Kendal commented. "You're doing splendidly. Can you spare two of your baker bees to loan Queen Zoey. It's a temporary assignment to help the 'kind bees' (that's the new name for the killer bee colony.) Your drones can train theirs."

"I'll get right on it, Kendal. A few of the guys are getting itchy."

"Why is that, Tee?"

"You met Mia. She's taking her maiden flight tomorrow. She'll be inspecting the likely prospects before she mates with any drones. They always cluster in the same location and wait for a new queen to show up. Most of my drone buddies plan to be there."

"What about you and Handy? Aren't you joining the others?" Kendal asked.

"No, Kendal. There are plenty of suitors without us taking up space. Besides, we have too much on our minds starting a training school for the local drones."

"Say, Tee," Kendal said. "There's a weather forecast predicting two days of rain, starting tomorrow morning. Will you get the word out to your hive and let the other hives know too?"

"Sure," Tee responded. *Two days of rain … hmm,* Tee thought. … That'll keep Mia home for two more days before she mates. The drones can concentrate on the baking business.

"Kendal, the sun's going down," Tee said. "If you want to get home before dark, you'd better get started."

"You're right, Tee. You guys earned an A plus for your achievements. I'll say bye for now."

As Kendal sailed home above the hives, squadrons of scouts ascended from the hives below. *Oh no,* he thought. *Not another chase!* As one squad flanked him on the right, a scout called, "Kendal, we're privileged to escort the King of the Bees to your home."

With 140 buzzing squads flying in close formation over the forest, animals and birds stopped their activities to stare. What an incredible sight flying high above them.

When he arrived at the old oak tree, Kendal thanked the scouts for their company, asking them to spread the news that heavy rain was due tomorrow.

## Chapter Twenty-Three

# Rains Down

A persistent pitter patter pounded on the old oak tree. Inside the hive, the drumming awakened Kendal. For the first time he discovered the hypnotic spell of falling rain; it sounded awesome. Those weather forecasters deserved a gold star this time. As he rubbed his eyes, Kendal ran for the hive entrance to experience rain for the first time in his life.

With a quick glance outside, Kendal didn't see one familiar object. Whatever was there was hidden behind sheets of falling water. When he dared glance up, he ducked automatically. The sky scared him. The clouds threatened to overflow and pour down on his head.

Kendal's head was spinning with random thoughts: Zoey is at work, laying eggs for the 'kind bees,' including a fertilized egg for their new queen. … Mia waits patiently for the rain to stop to go to mate. … Tee and his drone crew are busy in their bakery. … Poor Greeney is cooped up in a cocoon in the forest. Kendal hoped she was dry and protected from the drenching rain.

Over the next two days, Kendal solved every problem brought to his attention. Queen Victoria depended on his advice. Whenever possible, Kendal visited Zoey and Leah. They suggested he slow down. He needed time to think and be a bee.

What a grand way to live—respected by all … lots of friends … new things to plan and do. Kendal reached the pinnacle of success as 'King of the Bees.' Soon his picture would be plastered on the packages of miracle cakes throughout the world.

With all his blessings, Kendal knew something was missing. His birth meant the end of the royal line—number 304 pinned on Queen Zoey, was the last lapel pin ever to be awarded. No new retirees would arrive at the old oak tree hive to celebrate from this day on. A sad state of affairs, he confessed. Mixed emotions scrambled Kendal's brain.—what was that noise? He heard his name called. Queen Victoria was searching for him. She had another problem and needed his help.

The rain ended as predicted in late afternoon on the second day. Gushing rain stopped in the nick of time to let the afternoon sun begin a drying cycle. A rainbow spread its rich colors, kissing the earth in two places. That night, bees throughout the forest slept without interruptions or worries.

***

Before anyone else awakened, Kendal was up and out; he was anxious to fly north. He knew what he must do. As a thoughtful bee, Kendal wrote a note. He dropped it off at the 'kind bees' hive where Queen Zoey was staying as a volunteer.

Later, when Zoey opened the note, she read Kendal's words through her tears:

*Dearest Mother,*

*I made my decision after thoughtful consideration. It's both right and good that I pursue the new queen to mate with her. In this way I can ensure continuation of the greatest treasure ever bestowed on bees—the gift of the*

*power of royal longevity. After I mate, I know it will be my*
*turn to die; I'm ready.*

*I'll try to reach the old oak tree where I wish to be*
*buried. In this place my spirit will remain with all queens,*
*present and future. My last wish is you celebrate my life. I*
*am grateful for the life you gave me.*
*Love always, Kendal.*

"No, no!" Queen Zoey exclaimed. "My prince has decided his destiny. Such a tragedy! Such an unselfish deed! Bad things and good things do happen at the same time. I must pass the word."

As Kendal soared high above the trees, his excellent eyesight took snap shots of everything. He pretended to observe nature the way American Indians did. They appreciated the earth and its living creatures … they preserved their thoughts in writing.

With uncanny navigation skills, Kendal flew right for the area where drones hung around to mate, a hundred feet above the ground. In this same area, drones visited every year. They knew maiden queens might come cruising by to select a suitor. As Kendal arrived, he saw another drone coasting in front of him. In late afternoon, as Kendal circled the area; a new drone joined him.

"Are you Kendal?" the drone asked.

"Yes, I am," Kendal answered. "Have we met before?"

"No, Kendal. I'm learning baking from Tee. He described you. I knew you immediately by the color of your eyes."

"Baking is a wonderful occupation," Kendal said. It's just where I started—in bakery school."

"Kendal, are you planning to mate the maiden queen?"

"Yes. Why do you ask?"

"I'm sure you understand what that means. You'll die soon afterwards."

"Yes, I understand. But it's right and good, I do this," Kendal responded.

"I see the young queen flying this way," the other drone declared. "She flies too fast for me. I'm sure I can't catch her. You go ahead Kendal and pursue her. I'm going back to baking school."

As Mia flashed by, she waved. Kendal followed. He easily caught up with her. "Hi, Mia, do you remember me?"

"Of course, Kendal. I remember meeting you at the hive near Aidan's bedroom window. Tee introduced us. I hoped you'd come. We were meant for each other, don't you think?"

✳✳✳

Kendal hurt as he struggled to reach the old oak tree. His strength wavered. He tried ever harder. The trunk of the old oak tree was his final destination.

The forest behaved strangely; it turned off its sound system as Kendal continued his flight. He noted how birds perched on limbs of the trees, their heads hidden under their wings … squirrels sat up on their haunches, staring blankly at the sky … rabbits congregated, hesitant to bury themselves in their lairs … trees refused to rustle their leaves … the wind wept and slept quietly … bees rushed to their hives, the day's work unfinished.

Inside the old oak tree hive, the queen bees moved solemnly toward the entrance. They advanced sluggishly onto the limb. On a signal from Queen Victoria, they descended to form a circle on the ground at the base of the oak tree.

Back at Aidan's house the 140 hives emptied out. The bees reacted as they heard the news of Kendal's near death. They flew in tight formation, heading for the old oak tree.

Aidan ran indoors to tell his mother she must come and see what their bees were doing. Mrs. Bright, with Aidan and Kim, hurried outside and climbed into their wagon as they observed an unusual display of bee behavior. The swarms were heading south. Aidan thought the swarms spelled out, K E N D A L. He guessed they might be revealing the name of their new king.

Near the old oak tree, Queen Zoey landed with the colony of

'kind bees.' Rebecca arrived, leading Zoey's old colony. Near by, Tee, Handy and all the drones gathered to celebrate Kendal.

Aiming at a spot near the trunk of the old oak tree, Kendal stared. Who's there, he asked himself? His friend Spero the spider stood motionless on a new web in the exact spot Kendal chose to land. He anticipated Kendal's landing site. He weaved a blue silk web as soft as a comforter. Kendal strained to stay aloft long enough to hit the web, dead center as Spero schooled him on another occasion. Kendal hit, almost dead center.

The drones ran forward to encircle the web with Tee and Handy planting their feet in front of Kendal. Handy spoke first. "Kendal, I'm sad you're leaving us. Here, take my white fluffy hat, please."

"Thank you, Handy. I'll treasure it."—

Tee couldn't wait to speak to Kendal. "You gave your all, my dear friend. I heard the news. How are you doing, Kendal? Do you hurt? I wish you were staying. I have so much more to learn. You make us drones proud. I—"

"Slow down, Tee. How did you learn Yoodle's plans as a secret agent if you talked so much? Tee, I'm in pain but it's worth the price. You have such a skill, Tee; make sure you share it with others."

All the drones in Tee's party removed their white fluffy hats to salute their baker instructor and their king.

The queens processed by the web, paying their respects to their fallen king. They smiled affectionately. Queen Victoria stepped forward to give Kendal a kiss. She no longer wore her beard. "My queen, where's"—

"I removed the beard for good, Kendal, in honor of your many good deeds." Victoria leaned over to whisper words no one else heard.

The other queens retired to the top of a mound where they hummed their song in weeping and warbling tones; worker bees performed their waggle dance in honor of the First King of the Bees.

The Bright's wagon squeaked as it stopped with a lurch. Aidan jumped down with his beagle pal and ran to Kendal's side. He saw his drone friend was dying; he asked for the honor of burying him. Heydog wanted to help too. And so, the arrangements were made.

Aidan's mother moved forward with Kim hanging back. "Kim, I'll leave Kendal's picture right here on the spider's web. This is the picture to be used on packages of miracle cakes to be sold throughout the world."

Kim placed the picture close to Kendal. She was truly grateful for all he taught to Aidan and her.

Kendal tired fast. His Grandma, Queen Leah, leaned closer. She loved and admired Kendal; no words came. Zoey raised her voice as a preacher in the pulpit. She testified her son proved kindness and sacrifice are the most generous gifts of any heart. With flowing tears she placed the gold crown on Kendal's head and laid the folded emerald green cape on his chest.

"Mother," Kendal asked. "Please ask Handy to read this simple verse I wrote last evening. Handy needs the confidence of public speaking."

"Kendal, even now you're thinking of helping someone else … Handy, please read Kendal's words."

Handy picked up the scrap paper and read the verse:

> *Who am I to question why?*
> *To mourn the passing of another day.*
> *My life is written in the sky,*
> *The end prescribed is nature's way.*
> *I die a baker and fulfilled drone,*
> *Ready and willing to go back home.*

Queen Zoey gave in to her emotions. She started to sob and Queen Leah joined her.

"My dear mother … dear grandmother, I die so others may

live with royal longevity which is truly a gift. Dying is humbling. Also, it's rewarding. In giving, I am receiving … a joy neither a baker bee's hat nor a crown can match."

With great effort, Kendal replaced his crown with Handy's white fluffy hat, a reminder of his humble beginnings. All the drones in the vicinity placed their hats on their heads in solidarity as a growing baker bee fraternity. The time had come.

Even as the final moments arrived, the sunset darkened, blotted out by a large splash of muted color. A dark mass moved rapidly from the south As it came closer, the bees surrounding the site saw a contingent of thousands of monarch butterflies. Their wings were adorned in resplendent orange, laced with black veins and black fringes. Out of the formation, one butterfly peeled off from the group—landing at Kendal's side.

"Kendal, I'm here," the butterfly whispered in Kendal's ear.

"And you are?" Kendal asked, unsure who was speaking to him.

"I'm Greeney, the X caterpillar," she answered with a tender smile. "I brought all my sisters in migration to celebrate your passing to a well earned reward for your beautiful life."

Spontaneously, Greeney unfolded her wings and enwrapped them about Kendal in a welcoming hug. Greeney thought a halo crowned Kendal's head but it might have been pollen dust forming in the shape of a crown. It was the end.

Chapter Twenty-Four

# More To Come
# After The End

Today was the anniversary; nine months since Kendal died. In that time ... the fall fell ... winter waned ... spring dressed in new attire. Zoey and Leah huddled on the familiar limb where they often met to keep vigil over Kendal's grave.

With warm weather permitting outdoor activities, Kendal's burial site once again became a popular attraction. Out of respect, worker bees visited the site for a moment's silence; drones flew from afar to honor their buddy and their king; 304 queens shared stories about the royal prince who showed each of them personal kindness. Aidan and Kim stopped to update Kendal on what they were doing and to tell him they still missed him. With nature sparking new life, trees sprouted their leaves and birds fidgeted seeking the early worms.

On this anniversary, Queen Victoria joined Zoey and Leah at their well worn observation deck on the limb.

"Zoey, I've been thinking about this all winter," Victoria declared. "I want to share what I whispered to Kendal the day he died."

"We'd love to know," responded Zoey. "We wondered what you confided to Kendal."

Victoria unlocked her big secret. "I told Kendal I was entrusting him with the contents of my gold box keepsake. I gave him one tiny seed a worker bee gave me over 400 years ago. My worker bees found the seed in an exotic flower with six leaf clovers with yellow pigmentation; the flower was the source of our power of royal longevity. When I gave the seed to Kendal, I reminded him even a dormant seed is packed with power. Any seed can grow when it's planted in good soil. I wanted Kendal to take it with him wherever he was going."

"So that's what you treasured for over four hundred years!" exclaimed Leah. "We always wondered." …

… "What's that I hear?" Leah asked.

"I know the sound," Zoey answered. "It's the tell tale rattling of Aidan's wagon wheels coming our way."

Aidan hurried along with Heydog seated at his side in the front seat. "*Whoa*, Mosey." Aidan called. Mosey froze, glad to rest. Aidan climbed off the wagon carrying a memorial plaque dedicated to his friend. The sign was home made, stapled to a wooden stake. Aidan went directly for the spot, still covered by a few silky remnants of the blue web weaved by Spero nine months ago. Respectfully, Aidan hammered the sign into the soft ground.

Removing a pad from his pocket, Aidan read a note he printed on the first page.

*My dear drone,*
*    I came to tell you I think of you often. Your outfit was fit for a king. So I made you this sign. It says, 'First King of the Bees.'*

Zoey coasted down to say hello to Heydog who held a special place in her heart. Heydog's warning of the killer bees attack helped Kendal prepare for that horrible battle with Yoodle.

Heydog hoped he'd meet one of the queens. Mia and he were now friends. Whenever she found a spare minute, Mia came outside to chat with him, even in the rain. When she heard Aidan took his beagle to visit Kendal's resting place, Mia gave Heydog a message. Mia learned the story of royal longevity from Rebecca. So Mia wanted the queens to reserve a lapel pin numbered 305 for the special fertilized egg she planned to lay.

Later when Victoria heard Mia's request, she decided she'd better plan more bedroom space. Also, she ordered a new set of lapel pins starting with number 305 through 1,000.

As Zoey flew to the familiar limb above, Heydog nudged Aidan. He pointed with his nose to a fast moving cloud coming their way. A monarch butterfly migration was returning north to lay their eggs. One butterfly broke from formation. She landed gracefully at the grave site choosing an unusual flower to park on.

A familiar squeaky voice sang out. "Hi, Kendal. I'm here to celebrate my baker bee. You deserve this beautiful plant growing at your grave. It tells me all is well and your spirit remains the same in death as it did in life."

Victoria, Leah and Zoey focused their eyes on the unique plant. Victoria put on her glasses. "My goodness" she exclaimed. "Kendal's plant is budding flowers with six leaf clovers with yellow pigmentation. He's still working his wonders. Kendal is truly *awesome*, my sisters. With his passing, another story begins."

CPSIA information can be obtained
at www.ICGtesting.com
Printed in the USA
FSOW01n0311110117
29480FS